STORM

A SCI-FI ALIEN WARRIOR ROMANCE

THE SKY CLAN OF THE TAORI
BOOK FIVE

TANA STONE

BROADMOOR BOOKS

For Book Snob Sue, who loves the Taori and has been so supportive of my books!

xoxo

Tana

CHAPTER
ONE

Kaos

"You lead the way, Kalesh," I shouted to my leader as we huddled in the dank passageway, shadows snaking long fingers toward the group of females waiting to escape from the battle arena complex. Even though the air was cool in the subterranean passageways, my skin sizzled with heat and my chest heaved. Alarms shrieked overhead and heavy footsteps approached, telling me it was time to take our chance and run for the sky ship. "I'll bring up the rear."

Usually, Kalesh Naz would insist on bringing up the rear of the group and be the last to escape—just as he'd done when our sky ship was attacked by the Xulonians—but I knew he wanted to stay with the pink-haired female he called Tyrria. He'd clearly formed a bond with her, and he did not argue with me when I offered to be the last in the group.

As Naz's first officer who'd been serving under him across many galaxies and as many decades, I knew his mind almost as well as I knew my own. He could not leave his mate, but he felt responsible to ensure the safety of the female captives we'd liberated. If he was leading this mission with anyone else, he would not have agreed so easily, but my kalesh trusted me with his life, and knew I would value the lives of the females we were saving as dearly as my own.

I hitched in a breath to steady my racing heart, but my breaths escaped in pants and my flesh burned as I followed Naz and the women through another dark corridor, this one with a ceiling so low that my curved horns brushed the stone. Did my kalesh know how powerfully the Quaibyn was wracking my body? He must suspect that I was afflicted by the Taori curse, but we'd been too busy escaping from the dungeon and then freeing the females to discuss the state of my fever.

"I am the master of my being and the author of my fate," I said in a low voice, and through clenched teeth. The words were only for me, and I was grateful the females around me were too distracted to notice my mumblings.

I could not let my base desires alter my ability to fight like an honorable Taori warrior. I was a member of one of the strongest and most valiant warrior species in the universe. We had sacrificed our home world and all we knew to chase the Sythian swarm across the sky and save others from their cruelty. I'd been drenched in the blood of our enemy and carried the scars of many battles. I would *not* let something like a fever—even a cursed one—determine my fate.

I growled at this thought, provoking a startled look from one of the females nearest me as we emerged from the dark passageway. But both of our attention was swiftly drawn away at the bright light that beat down upon us and the sand that whirled through the air.

The tiny particles stung my face as I raised a hand to shield my eyes. I spotted a ship through the haze, then Naz's raised fist above the heads of the others. I lifted mine in answer, scanning the females in front of me to assure myself they'd all emerged from the underground corridor.

The kalesh took off in a run toward the ship and we all followed, with me bringing up the rear and tracking the slower females as they hiked up their dresses, gathered handfuls of the shimmery fabric, and ran. Naz raced up the lowered ramp of the ship as bellows erupted behind me. I chanced a glance over my shoulder, cursing when I saw thick-necked guards lumbering from the arena complex with blasters drawn.

Turning back to the ship, I barreled forward and hunched my shoulders low as I spread my arms wide and corralled the last females onto the ramp. I caught Naz's eye as he headed for the cockpit, giving him a nod to take off even though I was barely on board. There was no time to wait, as the blaster fire pinged off the steel hull of the vessel around me.

The wind buffeted my body and tossed my hair around my face as the sky ship lifted off the ground. The female with the brown curls who'd looked startled by my growls clung to me from behind as the sky ship rocked from side to side. There was no time to push her farther into the vessel, before I had to turn and snatch a weapon from the wall and return fire. Still, I curled one arm behind me to hold her steady as we rose into the air, the ramp slowly raising.

The kalesh's mate—the one he'd looked at as if she belonged to no one else in the universe—ran past us and toward the cockpit. Then the engines fired again, kicking the ship back, and the female behind me slipped, her feet skittering from beneath her she slid from my grasp and between my legs before I could tighten my grip.

Without a second thought, I dove for her as she tumbled down the lifting ramp. I reached her, snapping my own hand around her smaller one, but my momentum was too great, and we both flew out of the ship. I curled my body around hers as we plummeted through the air, the rushing wind and blowing sand making it impossible to scream.

The sky ship hadn't lifted very high from the ground, but I still closed my eyes and braced myself for impact on the hard surface of the flight deck, twisting my body so that I would hit first. Instead, we landed in a sand dune, rolling together down one side of the steep hill of sand before coming to a stop at the bottom.

I lay sprawled, face-up, as I attempted to regain the breath that had been knocked from me. The sun was brutal as it shone down on my skin, and the air was dry and hot, making it hard to take deep breaths.

The sound of the blaster fire was muffled, and as I pushed myself onto my elbows, I saw that we were hidden from the arena complex by the sand dune we'd rolled down. Tipping my head back, I saw the alien sky ship that held Kalesh Naz and the females I'd helped rescue. Instead of returning to the surface for us, the ramp clamped shut and it continued to ascend higher in the air.

"They're leaving!" The female struggled to her feet beside me, her face stricken as she gaped at the departing vessel. "They're leaving without us!"

Even though her screams couldn't yet be heard above the weapons fire and roaring of the engine, I couldn't risk her giving away our position. We might not be on the ship escaping, but at least we were not prisoners inside the arena. I would not be anyone's captive again.

I threw myself on the female, clamping a thick hand over her mouth and flattening my body to hers. "They will return for us."

Her eyes were wide as she stared up at me and struggled to push me off her.

The movements of her small body beneath mine sent unwanted pulses of pleasure through me and awakened the fever I'd been barely keeping in check. I closed my eyes, cursing in the ancient tongue of my ancestors as I tried to fight it off.

I could not be consumed by the Quaibyn. Not now. Not when I'd just been stranded on a barren, alien moon with a very scared, and very pretty, female.

The noises of the departing sky ship faded as did the sounds of blasters being fired. The creature under me went still as rough voices drifted to us from just on the other side of the dune. The cruel, heavyset guards were so close they'd only need to crest the sand to see us lying in the valley.

I didn't move from my position, my body covering hers and shielding her not only from view, but also from the biting sand and relentless sun. I held my breath and lowered my head so that it was almost nestled in her neck as I waited for the guards to return to the arena. There were a few dark grumbles and loud shouts of displeasure, but then they stomped away, their footfall fading as they left.

I let out a grateful sigh. In all the chaos of the sky ship taking off and kicking even more sand into the air, they hadn't seen us fall and land in the desert. We were alone, but we were no longer their captives.

I allowed myself a breath, inhaling the sweet scent of the female I was restraining and letting relief suffuse my body. Then I stiffened as a rumble built in my chest. We were alone. There was no one watching us. There was no one on the barren expanse of the alien moon to protect the small, frail creature but me.

I trembled with a possessive thrill mingled with thrumming desire, my flesh on fire. I'd encountered many females as my Taori ship had traversed galaxies, but none could be considered more desirable than the wide-eyed female with the soft curves barely concealed by her flimsy garment. The fact that she was so easily overpowered sent unwanted throbs of dark, dominant need pulsing through me. She was not a paid pleasurer who would spread her legs and moan for coin. Her favors would have to be earned—or taken.

I dragged the tip of my tongue up the length of her neck, unable to stop myself. She tasted as sweet as I imagined, her skin soft and the pulse in her neck trembling. Then I growled and felt her shudder beneath me.

I froze, my sense of Taori honor forcing aside my darkest desires as I felt her fear radiate into me. Had she realized that we were alone, and I was her only hope of survival? Or did she suspect that I was the beast on the alien moon she should most fear?

CHAPTER TWO

Kensie

I squeezed my eyelids together as I lay on the sand, which was harder than I'd expected for something that looked so soft. The impact of hitting the dune had knocked the wind out of me for a moment—even though the alien had taken the brunt of it—and after he'd pulled me back down and pinned me under his heavy body, I'd remained silent.

I'd braced myself in anticipation of our discovery by the guards, but I kept my eyes closed. I didn't want to see their tusked faces and their beady eyes as they jerked me up and dragged me back into the arena complex. I couldn't bear the thought of returning there without the other women who'd become my friends.

Tears stung the backs of my eyelids. Now my friends were gone. They'd escaped in the spaceship while I was still trapped on the Xulonian moon. I suppressed a sob as I thought of how close I'd been to leaving with them. If only I hadn't stumbled and fallen off the ramp.

Images of the horned alien leaping after me flashed through my mind. He'd sacrificed his own escape to keep me from falling from the ship alone, and he'd curled his body around me so that his back had been the one to hit the hard sand. He might be pinning me beneath him, with his head nestled in my neck, but that was only because the guards were still prowling nearby, their shouts and grumbled complaints rising over the swirl of the sand.

I allowed my body to relax slightly as the rough voices of the guards faded. They hadn't found us. Hope fluttered in my chest as their distinctive footsteps disappeared and the only sounds surrounding me were the whipping wind and the labored breathing of the alien pressing down on me. We might not have made it off the moon, but I was no longer a prisoner of the Xulonians. I didn't have a metal collar around my neck that could stun me or even kill me if I disobeyed an order, and I wasn't forced to attend to a series of alien fighters.

I released a breath. The only alien warrior I needed to concern myself with was the one who'd saved me, and he wouldn't hurt me. After all, he'd been one of the ones helping us escape.

I felt him exhale in relief, as well, then breathe in deeply. Before I could ask him to get off me since the guards were gone, he stiffened. His body went rigid, making me think maybe the guards hadn't all left. Had he heard something I hadn't? I remained motionless as his huge body trembled, but when his tongue traced a line up the length of my neck and he let out a primal growl, fear overtook any relief I might have felt.

A shudder wracked my body as I realized that the alien who had me trapped beneath him was burning up. I managed to work my hands up to his bare chest, which was slick with sweat that wasn't only from the blistering heat of the sun overhead. Was he ill? He was the one who'd been found on the moon's surface, after all. Maybe he'd been wounded and was going into shock. In any case, I needed to get him off me. He was so much bigger than me that if he lost consciousness while on top of me, I could actually suffocate.

I strained to push against the hard muscles of his chest. "I can't breathe."

His quick, shallow breaths stuttered, then he grunted and rolled off me. He moved away from me like a Berithian sea crab scuttling backward, and swiped a hand across his brow, which was streaked with pale sand and sweat. "Did I hurt you?"

I shook my head and pushed an errant curl from my face. Now that we weren't in a dim corridor or running toward a spaceship, I got a good look at my rescuer. Even though golden sand encrusted some of his long hair, it was black and swept back to reveal curling, horns that were striped with iridescent silver. A braid plaited along one side of his temple hung over one of his broad shoulders. Even though he wasn't standing, I knew from standing next to him in the tunnels that he towered over me and the long, fur-tipped tail that now lay motionless on the sand normally swished and quivered. Like the other of his kind who Tyrria had attended, his body was well-muscled, with dark ink covering almost all of it. Unlike the other one who wore a steel mesh sash across his chest, this alien had no such garment. But even as he hunched forward, I could see that the curling lines extending from his collarbone morphed into the shape of an open-mouthed skull that covered the entirety of his torso.

I fought the urge to touch the ink that was etched across ridged stomach muscles and vanished into low-slung, dark pants, but I couldn't stop myself from staring. When my gaze drifted lower to the pronounced bulge in his pants, my cheeks warmed. I remembered Tyrria's smile as she'd talked about the alien of his species she'd been attending. She'd clearly been enamored of him, even though I'd advised her not to get attached, and I wondered if the species' impressive anatomy had played a part in her devotion. Not that I'd blame her. There was something both brutal and compelling about the horned creatures with tails.

Another grunt from him made me glance up, my face burning as I realized he'd caught me gaping at his crotch. I looked pointedly away from him, brushing my sweaty palms down the front of my now-dirty dress that was covered in small rips. The garment that had been suitable inside a luxurious building seemed absurd now that I was outside in the elements.

He stood quickly, the graceful movement making me jump. "If you are unhurt, we should go."

"Go?" I managed to say, even though my throat was dry. I cast a glance around us at the barren desert. "Where are we supposed to go?"

He reached down and pulled me up with such force that I bumped into his chest, and he grabbed me by the shoulders to keep me from falling back. Tipping his head up to the blazing sun, he frowned, then looked down at me with an intensity that made me swallow hard. "We need to find shelter. We won't survive long out here without it." His gaze slid to the bare skin of my shoulders. "Your species is not designed for survival."

I bit back the urge to challenge him about what he knew of my species, but he was right. My skin could not withstand the white-hot heat of the sun for long, and humans had no ability to go for long periods of time without water, like the Narothens with their internal pouches. Then I digested the rest of his statement.

I swiveled my head. "Out here?" He didn't mean that we were leaving the only shelter in sight, did he? "I thought you said the ship would return for us."

His eyes burned with heat as he stared at me, finally gritting his teeth and tearing his gaze away. He closed a hand around mine and tugged me forward. "There is no doubt in my mind that my kalesh will find us, but we must be alive for that to happen. And preferably, not being held as prisoners."

His grip was so tight and his movements so forceful that I didn't have much choice but to follow. I cut my gaze to the dome of the arena as he pulled me deeper into the desert, worry tickling the back of my mind at the iron hold he had on my hand. Despite appearing unwell, he was still stronger than me. Was I giving up one captor for another?

CHAPTER THREE

Kaos

The female wrenched her hand from mine after we descended yet another sandy hill. I was so focused on striding forward and trying to ignore my hammering heart and blurry vision that it took me a few long strides to register that she'd pulled away from me. I whirled around, scowling, but my frown slipped when I saw her sagging shoulders and sweat trickling down her face. Her brown curls had gone limp and the sheer, colorful dress which had looked so alluring when we were inside the arena complex now hung from her in tatters.

"Where are we going?" She threw her arms wide. "I get that we wanted to escape from the guards, but I don't think they're hot on our trail."

I sucked in a breath of the thick, warm air, her words causing my own determination to deflate slightly Then I met her flashing eyes and was reminded of why I was so focused. The faster I moved, the less I could be distracted by my raging fever. Not that finding shelter and being in even closer quarters with the female would be any type of reprieve for me. But at least she would be protected from the harsh environment, even if she would not be entirely safe from all danger —namely me.

I scraped a hand through my hair, skimming my gaze over the barren landscape that was a mix of sand and rock. "We are looking for shelter." I waved in the general direction of a rocky ridge rising above the dunes in the distance.

She put her hands on her knees and peered at me. "How long were you out here before they found you and brought you to the arena?"

I twitched at the reminder. My memories were a jumble of sensations—the heat of the sand as I'd crawled from my escape pod, the coppery scent of blood as I'd tended to my wounds, the shimmering of the sand as I'd stumbled across the punishing terrain in an attempt to find water or shelter. "Not long enough. I didn't make it to the mountains."

She sank down to her knees and huffed out a breath. "What makes you think we will?"

I didn't want to admit that I had any doubts, although my advancing fever was not helping my overall outlook. I still believed that Kalesh Naz would return for us. My faith in my kalesh had not faltered. We just had to stay safe until then.

Black spots danced in front of my eyes and my fingers burned as if they were aflame. I did not have time to argue with a female who knew nothing of danger. With a guttural grunt, I strode to her, lifting her from her knees with one hand under her arm and reciting part of our battle litany under my breath to keep my mind distracted as I touched her. "We are the Taori. We are the Immortals."

"Immortal?" She eyed me with suspicion. "Is that why your crew mate didn't lose any of his fights in the arena? Can your kind not be killed?"

A reluctant smile escaped my lips, my stiff shoulders softening as I looked into her warm brown eyes. Her earnest question made we want to tell her everything, although I knew I could not. "It is what our army was called when we fought on our planet. We were called the Ten Thousand because of our vast number of warriors that were replaced as soon as one fell. That is why we were called Immortals." I glanced up at the harsh sun. "I assure you we can die like any other creature."

"And you're called Taori?"

I released her arm and nodded, the sizzle from her touch fading. "I am Kaos, first officer to Kalesh Naz of the Taori."

"Kensie." She extended one of her small hands. "I'm human."

I studied her hand—I should not touch her so much—before cautiously taking it. She moved our clasped hands up and down.

"It's how humans say hello," she explained, as she released my hand with a small smile. "One of the ways, at least."

The brush of her flesh sent fresh tingles up my arm, but I tried to ignore it. I made a rough noise in the back of my throat and started walking again, this time slower so she could easily keep pace with me. "I have heard of humans, but in my time you had not traveled beyond your solar system without help from the Drexians."

She fell in step with me, and her eyes widened. "Your time?"

I hesitated for a moment, but then realized that there was no harm in telling her the truth of our origin. She was not my enemy, even if my desire for her could be my undoing. "Our ship was sucked through a temporal wormhole and brought five hundred years into the future and thrust into the Xulonian's territory. They attacked us and destroyed our ship, and my Taori brothers and I were forced to escape in pods. Those of us that survived have obviously been scattered across the planet's surrounding moons."

"That's bad luck to be sucked into Xulonian territory. Everyone I know who ended up on one of their moons was kidnapped and forced to come here."

I grunted at this, rage churning in my gut. "You were abducted?"

Kensie's expression darkened. "I was traveling to a new colony with my family when our transport was attacked. Hettite slavers killed half of the passengers." She swallowed, clenched her jaw, and continued. "The rest were distributed among their recreational moons."

"And your family?"

She shrugged without meeting my gaze. "My parents were killed right away. I don't know what happened to my sister, but that was a while ago..." She let her words drift off.

My stomach twisted. "I am sorry. I share in the tears and sorrow for your fallen."

She jerked her head up, meeting my gaze with her brow furrowed. "You don't talk like other aliens, and I've met a lot of aliens in the arena."

I cocked my head at her. I did not believe she was a pleasurer, but I did not understand the purpose for her and the other females within the battle arena. "I understand why the Xulonians would abduct fighters for their arena, but you did not fight. Why were you taken?"

"They need women to take care of the winners." When I raised an eyebrow at this, she shook her head. "Not like that. At least, not usually. We're supposed to bring them food and tend to any wounds so they can fight again. I guess it's one of the incentives for the aliens thrown into the ring. There's less chance of an uprising if winning has rewards."

"But claiming you was not one of the rewards?"

Splotches of pink appeared on her cheeks. "Like I told Tyrria, most of the fighters were too worn out or wounded to try anything, and they rarely lasted more than a round or two before being defeated. Your buddy was rare."

"Kalesh Naz?" I almost laughed at her calling him my buddy. The leader I'd served under was more a father figure to be respected and obeyed without question than something so casual as a buddy.

She bobbed her head without noticing my amusement. "I've taken care of plenty of alien fighters and only a few lasted long enough to want more from me than good food and a long sleep." Pain flickered across her face. "Tyrria was lucky."

"Kalesh Naz is a brave and honorable Taori." My voice was little more than a reverent rumble as I spoke of my kalesh. "If he has taken her as his mate, she is very lucky."

Kensie looked up at me, a curious expression on her face as she opened her mouth. Before she could speak, the sand beneath our feet disappeared. She let out a small scream and I lunged for her hand, but we were both sucked under the ground.

CHAPTER FOUR

Kensie

My feet flailed beneath me as I was sucked under, and I grasped for purchase, but only found handfuls of air and sand as I fell. I squeezed my eyes shut as the desert swallowed me, feeling the brush of the Taori's hand as he reached for me. But then he was snatched away, and I was consumed by darkness and the rushing of sand in my ears.

When my feet hit something hard, pain shot up one leg and I yelped, spitting out grains of sand before I inhaled cooler air. I blinked rapidly, my eyes watering from the sand that had worked its way through my lashes and was now being flushed out by my spontaneous tears.

A groan from one side made me turn my head. Kaos was lying next to me, the shadowy shape of his massive form silhouetted by faint light from above. I tipped my head back, startled that the light was sifting through shafts that appeared to burrow up through the rock and sand above us.

I spat out what little spit I had left since it was filled with sand and made my mouth gritty. "What the hell?"

Kaos stood more quickly than I would have expected after our fall, and he assumed a battle stance as he pivoted to take in the entire subterranean chamber. "It is like Jerbon V."

I tried not to be annoyed at his nonsensical mutterings. Maybe the alien hit his head when he fell. "What's a Jerbon?"

"Jerbon V is a sand planet our sky ship encountered as we chased the Sythian swarm across the galaxies. They also had tunnels beneath the surface."

"Tunnels?" I swiveled my head to take in the dimly lit area, noticing for the first time that it wasn't a self-contained chamber, as I'd first assumed. Spokes extended from it in different directions. "Does that mean the moon is inhabited? By someone other than the Xulonians and guards?"

Kaos didn't look at me as he grunted. Was that a grunt yes or a grunt no? I blew out a breath. Were all Taori so spare with their words, or had I happened to be stuck with one who doled out words like they were a precious resource?

"Inhabited?" He finally answered my question with one of his own. "If these tunnels are any indication, yes."

"That's good news, right?"

Even in the low lighting, his brilliant blue eyes shone at me. "Not if the creatures who burrowed these tunnels are as hungry as we are."

My stomach dropped, and a chill danced across my bare skin. It hadn't occurred to me that the moon's inhospitable desert would contain creatures living beneath the sand, but now I couldn't help but imagine sounds of sand animals approaching. I tried to push myself up but fell back onto the ground with a cry.

Kaos was at my side, kneeling down before I could speak. "You are hurt." It wasn't a question, but from the harsh tone of his voice, it sounded more like an accusation.

I reached for my ankle, wincing as I touched it. "I might have twisted it when I fell."

"Your species is frail," he growled.

I shot him a dark look, although I couldn't argue that humans weren't weaker than the Taori. There was a reason few humans were put in the battle ring. "It's not like I did it on purpose."

A guttural rumble in the back of his throat was his only reply as he eyed my ankle without touching it. I tugged up the dingy fabric of my dress to expose more of my bare leg and see if my ankle was already swelling. He looked away and stood quickly with an angry huff of breath.

It was hard not to take his reaction personally, but my ankle was throbbing too painfully to care that the alien I was stuck with was repulsed by the sight of my bare leg. If he was anyone but a battle-honed Taori, I would have thought he was squeamish about injuries, but he had enough scars criss-crossing his own body to tell me that wasn't the case. His dismissive comments about humans only proved my point.

"Don't worry, buddy," I whispered so low he couldn't hear me as he paced restlessly around the space. "Horns and tails aren't my thing, anyway."

That wasn't exactly true. Before he'd made his distaste for humans clear, I'd been fascinated by his twitching tail and curious what the ridged stripes on his horn felt like.

Forget it, Kensie, I told myself, as I concentrated on breathing through the pain of my injured ankle. The last thing you need in your life is to get involved with someone who will probably die.

I'd lost enough people that I'd learned not to get attached, especially when it came to guys. I pushed aside the old ache I thought I'd suppressed, trying not to think of the human fighter I'd let myself get attached to when I'd first arrived in the arena. He'd been a space marine—tough and trained for battle, but with a sweet side he revealed after I'd helped him recover from a few fights. The lump in my throat soured as I thought about how naïve I'd been, and how I'd believed he had a chance to keep winning and stay with me. I swallowed down the bitter taste of regret as memories bubbled up of his broken body being brought to me, the guards' cruel laughter echoing in my head.

"Never again," I said, this time not keeping my voice at a hush. It didn't matter how intriguing the Taori was or that we were stranded together. I wouldn't feel that kind of loss again. Not for anything or anyone.

"I doubt your god or goddess can hear your entreaty."

I jumped at the low hum of the Taori's voice that snapped me from my mental wanderings. "I wasn't praying."

He craned his head over his shoulder to meet my gaze, his iridescent eyes flashing heat beneath the icy blue shimmer. "Maybe you should."

CHAPTER FIVE

Kaos

I swung my head away from her, forcing myself to focus on the problem at hand.

As if she wasn't part of the problem, I thought, as a snarl escaped my lips. How did I break free from the alien battle arena and end up trapped beneath the sand with a fragile, wounded female? The last thing I needed was to be back on the punishing alien moon, but at least when I'd been stranded before, I'd been alone. There had been no one who could be hurt by my burgeoning fever but myself.

I curled my hands into fists, fighting the storm building inside me and trying to control the curse that couldn't be tamed. Now I was burdened with a creature who not only provoked the heat and fury of the Quaibyn, but who was injured and needed my protection to survive. I cut my gaze to the tunnels that told me we were not alone under the sand, my tail twitching in anticipation. I'd told Kensie that she should pray to her gods, but it was I who needed the power of the universal energy to save me from my fate. And to save her from me.

I exhaled a heavy breath before arching my neck to peer up then I stretched my arms up as high as they would go. My fingertips brushed the rough, damp ceiling but there was nothing to grasp. I bent my legs and leaped up. This time, my palms smacked the ceiling and sent sand sifting down on my head, but there was no way to hoist myself up and out.

"I don't think we can crawl back up."

I agreed with the female, but I didn't want to tell her she was right. I stalked beneath the sand, squinting up and searching for where we'd fallen through. I jumped up, bracing my hands inside an opening and pulling myself up by sheer force. Even with all my strength, I could only manage to get partway up a vertical tunnel that was surprisingly slick, and my fingers slipped as I tried to find purchase. The crevice through the sand was narrower than I'd expected, considering both of us had fallen through, and as I wedged myself higher I brushed against sand, which filtered down onto my head. How could I push through the sand to reach the surface, and how would I bring Kensie with me?

Defeated, I dropped back to the ground, landing in a crouch, and letting my head fall between my shoulder blades. "We cannot get out the way we came in."

The human made a noise that sounded both self-satisfied and irritated. I ignored it, reminding myself why I'd avoided entanglements with females for so long.

There was a reason I was so good at my role of first mate to the kalesh. I was devoted to nothing as much as I was to my duty and to my sky ship. My heart belonged to my Taori brothers and to our mission. Females were nothing but a distraction that would pull my focus, much like the injured female did now.

A dormant sound of derision rumbled my chest as I resumed pacing the cavern, keeping my gaze away from the creature on the ground. She might seem small and harmless, but I knew all too well how even the sweetest flowers had thorns. I flinched at the painful memories that twisted in the back of my brain, but fighting the Quaibyn made it difficult to keep old wounds from opening. I did not have the strength to battle my fever and the toxic swirl of images crowding my mind.

I stopped and leaned my hands against the cool damp walls, my palms sizzling from the contact. The last thing I needed was to think of my first love on Taor, the one who'd cast off my affections when she'd drawn the attention of my older brother. I'd believed her to be as in love as I was and not to be swayed by the lure of a first born's status and inheritance. I'd been wrong and betrayed by both my love and my brother.

The taste of bile in the back of my throat was sharp as I remembered disavowing them both and swearing my allegiance to Kalesh Naz and the mission to defeat the Sythians. I'd vowed to myself I would never allow anyone to have power over my heart again. So far, I hadn't come close to breaking my vow.

I scowled as I stole a look at the human. Being trapped with a hungry beast would be preferable to my current situation. At least I could fight the beast and experience the rush of battle. Taking care of such a vulnerable creature—and one who triggered my fever—was worse than torture.

"Can you stop doing that?"

I looked away quickly, dropping my hands from the wall and turning to face her. "Stop what?"

"Looking at me like I did this on purpose." She glared at me with an impressive fury for one so small and weak. "I'm not the one who wanted to run off into the desert so we could die of starvation or fall into some sand creature's lair to get eaten."

"You would have preferred to stay in the alien arena as their slave?" I spat out, the anger in my own words startling me.

"I wasn't a slave." Her voice was now shrill. "And, yeah, living in luxury and eating regular meals wasn't so bad compared to this. At least I wasn't at risk of dying."

"You were a captive." I waved a hand at her, aware that my tail was swishing wildly behind me. "They had collars on your necks to punish you."

Her gaze dropped. "I didn't say I was okay with all of it."

Even though her tone was no longer tinged with anger, my own rage was at a boiling point. I crouched next to her, lifting the gauzy fabric of her dress and letting it flutter back down. "You would rather be forced to dress like a pleasurer?" I touched a finger to her neck where the mark from the metal collar remained. "You would rather be treated like an animal than be free with me?"

Her breath hitched in her chest as I jerked my hand back, the contact with her skin sending a jolt through my body. Her eyes had darkened, and they flashed at me in challenge through the dusky light. "The only thing I know about you is that you're big, intense, and way too bossy for your own good. How do I know you're any different from any of the fighters I had to attend in the arena or the guards who told me what to do? So far, I'm still getting ordered around, only this time there's no bathing pool or wine to take the edge off the fact that I'm not in control of my own life."

Her last words trembled, draining the heat from the response that was on the tip of my tongue.

I released a long, gravelly sigh. "I have no wish to control you. I thought I was saving you."

She was silent for a moment before letting out a sigh of her own. "I guess you did, although it would have been nice to have been given a choice."

I flinched, remembering the last female who'd made a choice and hadn't chosen me. I stood brusquely and crossed my arms over my chest. "As soon as my kalesh returns for us, you will be free of me, and I will be free of you."

"I didn't say I—" Kensie started, but I rushed to her and clamped a hand over her mouth to silence her words.

Her eyes were wide as she stared at me, obviously confused by my action—until she heard the scraping sound emanating from deep inside one of the tunnels—and coming closer.

CHAPTER SIX

Kensie

The huge hand pressing over my mouth startled me, but not as much as the way Kaos' body tensed and his tail went still, only the dark tip vibrating. I swallowed my explanation, forgetting that I was going to tell him I hadn't meant I wanted to be rid of him. Our argument seemed ridiculous once I heard the scraping sound echoing down one of the dark tunnels.

Fear slid down my spine, and I shuddered. What kind of creature was approaching?

Instinctively, I tried to stand, but the pain in my ankle almost dragged a gasp from my throat. Luckily, the Taori's hand still covered my mouth and muffled any cry. He met my gaze, locking eyes with me intently. I knew without him making a sound that he wanted me to stop moving and stay quiet.

I nodded, and he slid his palm from my mouth, silently scooping me up in his arms. I bit back a sharp inhalation from the pain and, instead, I held my breath as the massive alien carried me from the chamber. I don't know why I was so surprised that Kaos moved stealthily, but I marveled at how quick he was without making a sound. He might look like a hulking beast, but he moved like a cat.

Almost as soon as we left the large chamber and entered one of the offshoot tunnels, the faint light vanished, and we were engulfed in a darkness so complete I couldn't even see my own arms wrapped around Kaos's neck. The scraping sound had grown fainter, though, and I was confident his instincts had been right when he'd quickly chosen our path. For the first time since he'd dragged me onto the desert, I was glad to have the Taori on my side.

Although Kaos moved briskly, he wasn't running. Still, his bare chest, which I was pressed up against, burned like he was on fire. Maybe he'd been more affected by the scorching sun than I'd noticed. The tattoos did cover skin, but that didn't mean they provided protection. My own lighter skin was warm to the touch, and I had no doubt it would develop a burn later.

I didn't mind the heat from his exposed flesh, since the air in the underground tunnels was cool and dank, and I found myself resting my cheek on his chest to keep from shivering. As soon as I'd gotten comfortable with the darkness and my position pressed against Kaos, he stopped abruptly and nearly dropped me on the ground.

I stifled a yelp, not sure if the creature could hear us or if there were other creatures who might scuttle after any noise. But the only thing surrounding me was silence, and the only thing interrupting that was Kaos' rhythmic breathing. Hearing him breathe kept me from panicking since I couldn't see a thing and he'd set me on the ground and stepped away.

"Kaos?" I whispered, the sound barely audible.

His only answer was to kneel beside me, the heat from his body and the bump of his knee telling me he was almost on top of me. I lifted a hand to his chest, my fingers slipping on the slickness of his flesh. Sweat was running down him in rivulets, and his breathing had become shallow and fast. Did he sense something I didn't? Did he know we were about to be attacked?

My own pulse trembled, and my mouth went dry. I slid both hands to his shoulders, gripping them for balance in case I needed to stand—or at least try to. "What's wrong?"

Kaos took my hands in his and removed them from his shoulders, his hands holding my wrists firmly. "Do not."

Do not *what*? My mind raced through the possibilities. Do not talk? Do not try to stand? Now he was scaring me. His voice sounded strained and raspy, and his hands shook as they held mine. Something was wrong, but I didn't know what.

I almost cursed at myself out loud. Why had I tried to leave the arena complex? Why had I tried to change my fate? Hadn't I learned that hope was dangerous? Hadn't life taught me that wanting more was only the path to more pain?

I should have stayed where I was and accepted that my life would be spent as a prisoner of the Xulonians. It could have been worse. Being an attendant to the arena fighters hadn't been so bad. I could have lived a decent life there. At least I wouldn't be in a dark tunnel underground, wondering whether I was about to be ripped to bits by some unseen sand beast. My only comfort was that I wouldn't be able to see it when it happened. I might not know the Taori well, but I didn't know if I could bear to see him torn apart.

I closed my eyes as if to shut out even more than the darkness. Let it be quick, I thought. Just don't let either of us suffer. Before I could choke out a sob of regret that I was going to die in the dark with a virtual stranger and no one would ever know what happened to me, a low growl made the hair on the back of my neck stand on end.

It took me a moment to realize that it wasn't coming from somewhere deep in the bowels of the tunnels. It was a velvety soft sound that was curling around my belly and sending heat pulsing between my legs, and it was coming from Kaos.

His hands still held my hands, but he slid me so that my back bumped the firm wall and pinned my wrists over my head. Before I could ask him what he was doing, his body was cocooning me, the heat roiling off his bare skin and into me like waves. Even if I'd realized what he was doing, I couldn't move from the force and weight of him.

A hopeful thought fluttered in my mind. Maybe he was protecting me from some incoming threat I couldn't detect. Then his head was at my neck, breathing in so deeply that that thought evaporated instantly. His lips moved against my skin, whispering dark, silky words I couldn't understand as he inhaled again, his body going taut.

He was scenting me. The thought unfurled ribbons of terror within me, and I bucked against him, struggling pointlessly against the alien who was so much bigger and more powerful than me. How had he gone from looking at me like I was an irritant and talking about being rid of me, to pinning me to the wall?

Fire danced in my veins as his tongue tickled my throat, and for the briefest moment I wondered if his species was cannibalistic. I knew almost nothing about the Taori, except that the one who was currently licking my neck seemed to have a multiple personality disorder. One moment he despised me and the next he was running his tongue up my neck. I clenched my jaw as I fought against the sinful heat his touch was provoking, telling myself that his mouth did not feel good on my skin, and that I couldn't feel how hard he was everywhere, even though my eyes were almost rolling back into my head. I bit down hard on my bottom lip to snap myself from the unwanted haze of desire his touch had unleashed on me.

"Kaos!" I said his name sharply, but I didn't raise my voice about a furtive whisper. "First officer of Kalesh Naz of the Taori!"

He jerked back and released my hands, moving away from me as fast as he'd pinned me to the wall. Even through the dark, I could hear the agony in his release of breath. "I should not be here with you. I have put you in danger."

"By dragging me into the desert?" I rubbed my wrists. "I think we already established that."

"No. I have put you in danger by exposing you to my fever."

Fever? So, my suspicions had been right. Well, this day was just getting better and better.

CHAPTER SEVEN

Kaos

"Fever?" The female's voice rose an octave. "You're sick?"

I eyed her through the dark, my heightened visual acuity making it possible for me to see her in gray tones as she sat against the tunnel and rubbed her wrists. A pang of regret arrowed through me, as I thought of how it had been me who'd held her wrists tightly enough to hurt her. Well, not entirely me, although the distinction sounded weak even to my own internal judge.

I breathed in the slightly fetid smell from deeper in the tunnels, grateful that at least the putrid air was cool and was helping me regulate my feverish body heat. I raked both hands through my hair, both sweat and the grit of the sand coating my palms. I brushed my fingers along the ridges of my horns, the sensation a comforting touchstone, despite my horns usually provoking arousal.

"It is not a traditional fever," I told her. "You cannot catch it."

Her shoulder sagged in relief. "Then why did you say you'd exposed me to danger by exposing me to your fever? Correct me if I'm wrong, but doesn't that mean it's transmissible?"

I suppressed the urge to growl my response. I had said that, and clearly scared her. Now that I wasn't touching her, my heart no longer raced, and the sweat had stopped rolling off me. The black spots had stopped cavorting in front of my eyes and the thoughts in my mind weren't a furious torrent that made my head ache.

"My words were hasty." I kept my voice low. I couldn't hear any sounds of other creatures, but I didn't want to alert them to our hiding place. "My fever isn't contagious, but it is dangerous."

"Is it deadly?" She dropped her voice. "Could you die?"

"It is deadly, and I could die, but not before I would go mad and inflict a great deal of damage."

Kensie didn't respond to this, but I could see her jaw drop as she wrapped her arms around herself, probably to ward off the chill and to put up some meager form of self-protection. I almost smiled at the action, knowing it would do little to protect her from me.

"You do not know much about the Taori?" I asked.

She shook her head then added, "Not really. Tyrria didn't share much about your friend. I only knew what I saw. You're big, you're tough, and you're trained to fight."

I let myself slide down the wall until I was sitting across from her. "The Taori are skilled warriors, but we are also cursed."

She blinked a few times. "Did you say cursed?"

I allowed myself a long exhale. "I won't bother you will the entire tale, but the males of our species are afflicted with what we call the Quaibyn, a mating fever."

"I've heard of species who have mating fever."

"Our mating fever is particularly virulent. It occurs only once every decade or so, but it consumes us with fever, endows us with extra strength and physical abilities, and makes us mad with lust."

"Literally mad? If you don't cure it, you go crazy?"

I shivered unconsciously at the prospect of delving into madness. "Not only will we go mad if we don't quench our fever, but we also eventually morph into violent creatures who destroy and devour anything in their path, the very creatures we have sworn to destroy."

Kensie was quiet for a moment then she shook her head. "That's a pretty bad fever. You're worried that when you turn into this creature, I'll be in danger?"

I didn't speak. How did I tell the female that I would be a danger to her long before I morphed into one of the horrific Sythians? Before the madness overtook me and all my rational thoughts and memories were obliterated, I would lose control of all inhibitions and self-control. The fever's carnal lust would make her irresistible, and not even my deeply instilled sense of Taori honor would be able to stop my primal, animalistic desires.

I was torn between my determination to save the human, and the knowledge that I might be more dangerous than any alien guard or battle arena. My intentions when I'd jumped from the ship to save her had been honorable, but the more I was with the female, the harder it was to keep my fever in check.

"Wait," Kensie said. "Is that why you pinned me against the wall and were smelling me?"

My face heated even though my fever had subsided. Shame simmered within me, and I bowed my head. "You must understand that I would never touch you if I wasn't being affected by the Quaibyn."

"Thanks, I think."

"It isn't that you aren't desirable, but I have never had any intention to take a mate. My loyalty is to my Taori brothers and our mission. Females are a useless distraction I have never wanted or sought out."

"You really know how to make a girl feel special," she muttered, tilting her head. "Who hurt you so bad you swore off women?"

I huffed out a breath, frustrated that she was focusing on the wrong thing. "That doesn't matter."

"So, there was someone." Her voice softened. "Don't worry. I get it. I've been burned before and have sworn off love for good, too."

This made me pause. She felt the same way? Then I remembered the arena and her job there. "I imagine attending so many males might make you wish to never see one again."

"It wasn't that." She went quiet for a moment. "Before I understood that the fighters weren't meant to survive for long, I formed an attachment. It isn't a mistake I intend to make again."

I could not suppress my curiosity or the twinge of jealousy that flickered inside me. "This attachment you formed...?"

"He died," she said brusquely. "Like I said, I won't make the mistake of falling for anyone who could die again."

I did not remind her of the obvious fact that everyone died eventually, even aliens who lived for a millennium expired at the end of their long lives. Her sharp tone told me to remain quiet.

She took a deep breath. "What about you? I told you mine, now you have to tell me yours."

"I am not familiar with this rule. Is it a human one?"

"Tit for tat? I think it's universal."

I frowned, confused by the words my universal translator implant fumbled over. I understood tit, but what was a tat? "You want my tat?"

She laughed and the lilting sound echoed around us. "Don't flatter yourself, big guy. Who made you swear off women? Ex-wife? Ex-girlfriend?"

Long-held hurt rushed to the surface as I choked out the words. "My intended mate switched her affections to my elder brother."

She drew in a sharp breath. "Ouch. That's rough."

I grunted. The last thing I wanted was her sympathy or to be discussing our past heartbreaks. Didn't she understand the danger she was in or how I was powerless to control it? "None of that matters now. It doesn't matter if I want nothing to do with females or if you have sworn never to love again. Not when it comes to the Quaibyn. As much as I do not want it, I fear that my carnal urges will soon overpower my true wishes."

She shifted, straightened, and rearranged her arms so they were folded tightly over her chest. "Let me get this straight. You dragged me out onto this godforsaken planet so that we're all alone and now you tell me that being alone with me is making you have urges you might not be able to control even though the last thing you want is to touch me?"

I didn't answer right away. When she phrased it like that, I did not sound like the honorable Taori I wished to be. Or much of a protector. I cursed the Quaibyn, which had clearly affected my judgment in bringing her with me, and I cursed ever getting mixed up with another female.

I should have learned my lesson ages ago on Taor, when I'd

been betrayed. Females were nothing but a cause of conflict and agony. I'd been blessedly free of both since leaving Taor, so why had I subjected myself again?

Even though she was in shadow now, it was impossible to ignore the fact that she was small and fragile. Her kind didn't possess scales or horns or claws. She had no way to defend herself against enemies. Even if I'd made a massive error in saving her and bringing her with me, I couldn't abandon her now. She'd never survive on the hostile, alien moon alone. Even a Taori in the throes of mating fever was preferable to dying of thirst or being torn apart by a sand creature. At least, I hoped she would see it that way.

"I swear to you that I will do everything in my power to keep you safe until we are rescued," I said solemnly. "Even from myself."

She eyed me as she considered my words. "I guess I don't have much choice if I ever want to leave these tunnels."

I stood, resolved to find our way back to the surface so we could be rescued as quickly as possible. The sooner I was free of the burden of the female, the better.

Then, the tunnel we were in shuddered as if it was alive, and the walls started to contract around us.

CHAPTER
EIGHT

Kensie

"What was that?" I thrust my arms wide as the ground shifted beneath me. How were the tunnels moving? "Is this an earthquake?"

The prospect of being buried alive on an alien moon sent tendrils of fear curling around my heart, and I tried to scramble to my feet. I didn't care that my ankle throbbed with pain. I wasn't especially claustrophobic, but the thought of the tunnel collapsing on top of me was enough to make me push the pain from my mind. Being in the dark didn't help, and I swallowed a sob as I tried to steady myself with a hand on the wall, which seemed to be closing in on me.

Then Kaos' arm was looping around my waist, and he was lifting me up into his arms. "It isn't an earthquake."

Despite our fractious conversation about the mating fever

that seemed suspiciously like an excuse for bad behavior, I was grateful for his presence. His strong arms holding me close didn't scare me. In fact, they were comforting in a way that a male's touch hadn't been in a very long time.

I shook off those thoughts as sand fell from above and strange noise emanated from deeper within the system of tunnels. "Are the tunnels collapsing?"

The Taori grunted as he listed to one side after a particularly hard jolt, but he didn't loosen his grip on me. "These aren't tunnels."

The chill that had been dancing across my bare flesh turned to ice. Kaos stumbled forward as more groans came from around us and the tunnel that apparently wasn't a tunnel tipped sharply up. I was too terrified to ask what it was if it wasn't a tunnel, but I had a very bad feeling.

Kaos staggered to the side, and we bumped into one of the walls. I pressed a hand to the damp surface, noticing that it was almost spongy. It certainly wasn't rock or hardened sand, like I'd originally thought.

"We weren't being chased by a sand creature, were we?" I asked, as Kaos righted himself and took long strides up the inclined passageway.

A guttural noise was his only response. His muscles were straining as he attempted to get both of us up the increasingly sharp slope, and his breaths were short and fierce.

"We're inside the creature," I murmured, more to myself than to him, the truth of our situation hitting me. Then I slapped his chest. "Put me down."

A dark rumble slipped from his lips between heavy breaths. "You cannot walk."

I wriggled in his arms. "It will be easier for you to keep your balance if you have your arms free. You can still mostly carry me, but I can hop beside you and let you have at least one arm free."

He hesitated for a beat but then the tunnel gyrated and sent us slamming into the wall. He groaned from the impact as I yelped.

I took his face in both of my hands even though I couldn't see him. "Trust me. We'll be able to move faster this way."

With a dark sound that expressed both his frustration and acceptance, he swung me down and put me on the ground with as much care as he could as the passageway—or inside of the creature—continued to undulate around us.

I winced from the pressure on my ankle and was glad we were in the dark and I didn't have to worry about putting on a brave front. Sometimes it was easier to push through the pain if you could grit your teeth and make faces while you did it.

"If we're inside a creature, it must be enormous," he said. "I doubt it's aware of our presence."

"If it's so big, we probably aren't the only creatures in here."

Kaos growled, clearly not happy with this idea. "At least we aren't in the stomach, although I suspect these tunnels lead there."

I gulped, tasting the sharp bite of my own fear. "Then we need to keep going up." A shudder wracked my body. "Toward the mouth."

Kaos hooked one arm around my hips, lifting me off the ground as he strode forward. I was right. We could move faster without him having to carry me. Despite the pitch blackness, he seemed to sense the dimensions and direction of the tunnel, propelling us forward and keeping us from being hit by the contracting and expanding walls.

I kept one hand extended to the side to prevent Kaos from

bumping the sides of the tunnel and another clamped over my nose. The stench from the creature we were inhabiting had only grown more powerful, and my eyes watered from the acidic scent that clung to the air. Common sense told me that I was smelling stomach acid meant to dissolve organic matter like me, but I forced myself to brush aside images of falling into a churning, alien gut.

"What are the chances this thing has sharp, pointy teeth?" I asked, as I did my best to hobble quickly.

"I have encountered few alien beasts without teeth."

I groaned. "I guess Taori don't believe in sugarcoating the truth?"

"Lying?" He readjusted his grip on my waist as the tunnel tilted to one side. "If I believed in lying I would not have told you that I was afflicted by a mating fever that made me want to tear your clothes off you."

I swung my head to him even though I still couldn't see anything. "You didn't mention wanting to tear off my clothes."

I gave a small scream as the passageway tightened around us so that I bumped my head, and I felt Kaos hunch over. The pulsating movement sent us both skittering back a bit.

"I don't think my condition is our main concern," he said through gritted teeth, as he pulled me forward.

I couldn't argue with him. If we made it out of the inside of the alien creature, I wasn't even sure I cared about the Taori's mating fever. "You're right. If we escape from here, I'll be so happy to be alive and not digested by a giant sand beast that I might tear *your* clothes off."

He twitched at this but didn't respond, which was probably for the best. The fumes from inside the creature were making me lightheaded, and I was babbling.

Shut up, Kensie. Do not embarrass yourself before you die.

I twisted to look at Kaos again and this time I could make out the silhouette of his horns and the long hair falling across his shoulders. His jaw was tight with exertion and his shoulders bunched. I almost gasped when I realized that faint slats of light were filtering down from above, which meant we were close to the surface—or the mouth of the beast.

I had the strangest burst of affection for the huge alien who was risking himself to help me. There was no question that he could have already freed himself from the animal if I wasn't with him. But he'd never given any indication that leaving me behind was an option, and for some bizarre reason, I believed he would save me. Even if he had confessed that he was as dangerous as anything on the alien desert—although that was before we'd realized we were inside a sand creature, I reminded myself. I squeezed his shoulders, smiling at him even as his focus was on the terrain ahead.

He cut his gaze to me quickly, one eyebrow quirking. My pulse quickened as his electric blue eyes locked on me, the manic heat that had burned behind them replaced with an intense curiosity that was almost as unnerving. Then the tunnel contracted so tightly we were smashed together, our foreheads bumping painfully, and then, in the next heartbeat, we were expelled in a shower of sand and blistering sunlight.

CHAPTER NINE

Kaos

The force of being blasted from the creature made me lose my hold on Kensie as we both flew through the air and tumbled onto the sand. Her shriek told me she'd also been thrown clear and then I was rolling down a dune with her, our limbs entangled as we finally came to a stop at the bottom with her flopped on top of me.

Something sticky coated my skin, and I cringed as I imagined why we'd been so abruptly purged from the insides of the creature.

"Did we get sneezed out?" Kensie tried to push off me, but her hands slipped on my bare chest, and she fell back down, her own gooey chest hitting mine with a splat. She groaned, turning her head, and spitting a mouthful of something on the sand next to me. "This might actually be worse than being inside it."

I remained on my back as she struggled to get off me, wiggling and sliding around like an armless Cartov beetle. I was catching my breath from the impact on the sands and trying not to react to her practically gyrating on me, but since she was doing such a convincing impression of a struggling insect, it wasn't hard to keep my arousal at bay. Soon, my chest began to rumble with uncontrollable laughter.

She stilled. "Are you laughing at me?"

I shook my head even as a low, gravelly laugh burst from me. Kensie glared at me but then her own lips started to quiver. She slapped my chest, slipping again and sliding off my body and onto the sand.

"This isn't funny," she managed to gasp through her laughter.

I sat up and gazed at her. Golden sand was plastered to the female's sticky skin so that she looked like she was some kind of sand creature, herself. I pressed my lips together to contain the mirth that was threatening to overtake me.

She huffed out a reluctant laugh and smeared a hand across her sand-encrusted forehead. "I guess we've reached the laugh or cry portion of the day."

I stood and extended a hand to her. "Since we didn't get devoured and digested by the creature, I think we deserve a moment of celebration."

Kensie waved one hand weakly in the air. "Hooray. We were sneezed to safety."

I took a moment to eye her ankle as she leaned on me. "Did you suffer further injury when we were thrown free?"

"Shockingly not. I landed mostly on you." She rubbed one hip. "Not that there's anything soft on you." She seemed to realize her words as her cheeks flushed and she glanced away from me. "Not that you're hard. I mean, not in that way. The rest of you is definitely hard, but I didn't mean...crap."

I watched the color in her cheeks deepen with fascination. I'd never known a species to betray their emotions through their skin, but her embarrassment was clearly making her face mottle pink. It made me want to see which other emotions made her skin flush, and if she turned different colors, or only pink. Then I wondered what color her skin would turn if she was in the heat of passion, and my pulse quickened.

Just because she is laughing now does not mean she is not still angry at you for dragging her into such a mess, I told myself. One thing I knew about females, their moods could shift faster than the winds during a storm. I ignored my thickening cock, focusing on her matted hair to try to keep my own desires in check. Even covered in beast goo and sand, I had to fight the urge to touch her.

Kensie seemed to sense my hungry gaze on her, and she cleared her throat as she cut wary eyes to me. "Are we really back on the desert where we started?"

I scanned around us, shaking my head. "We might need to thank whatever creature that was. It brought us almost to the base of the rocky range."

She peered beyond me, her eyes widening. "You're right." She cut her gaze over her shoulder. "That thing must travel fast under the sand."

My stomach twisted with unease. "Since I doubt we were sneezed out on purpose, I suggest we get off the sand as quickly as possible in case it returns."

Kensie gnawed the corner of her bottom lip, her gaze darting to the sand at our feet, as if it could open up and swallow us whole again. "I'm ready to hobble."

I scoffed at this, scooping her up into my arms. "This will be faster."

She didn't protest. Instead, she coiled her arms around my neck to keep from being jostled as I ran with her. The faster I pumped my legs, sand kicking out behind me, the easier it was to ignore the freshly blooming heat in my core and the sinful fire skimming over my skin. Running was significantly less comfortable for the hard bar of my cock that was straining against my snug pants, but I ignored it as I pinned my focus on the rocks rising ahead of me.

Shelter was my goal. We needed cover from the punishing heat and the deadly creatures roaming under the sand, and I needed a place to put her that wasn't in my arms. As natural as it felt to carry her lithe body, I knew the more I touched her, the harder it would be to suppress my feverish hunger. And I had to keep the fever from consuming me and my Taori honor.

There were no more holes in the sand, and soon I was running up hardpacked ground that wound into the peaked hills. Sharp, jagged edges jutted into the white-hot sky, making the rocky area look just as deadly as the desert, but I knew it was our only hope of respite. There had to be a cavern or overhang within the range.

I tipped my head back. If I could get high enough, I could send a signal to Kalesh Naz when he returned to orbit. It would be easier to spot the ship returning from a higher altitude, anyway. My heart thumped in rhythm with my footsteps, as I thought of my kalesh returning. There was no part of my being that believed he wouldn't return to rescue me.

"Um, Kaos."

Kenzie's worried tone made me look down, but not before my foot was already slipping down a steep, rock slide. I landed hard on my ass, but managed not to drop the female, who screamed as we catapulted down the sloped rock that twisted through a narrow crevice in the cavern. She hunched her body tight to mine as my shoulders scraped the rock on either side, and I flinched and curled around her. Tightening into a cocoon around her only made us go faster, and even I closed my eyes as we whipped around a bend and into the air.

I repeated the Taori lament for the dead in my head in anticipation of our bodies slamming against the side of the rocks or landing violently at the bottom. But the impact never came, and soon, we were plunging into a pool of water.

I gasped at the shock of the water, sucking it into my mouth and kicking up so I could cough wildly in an attempt to spit it out. Kensie resurfaced beside me, also coughing up the cool liquid.

I gaped at our surroundings, the stripes of the rock were like waves cut into the stone and created a spectrum of rust, ochre, and brown. Water trickled down from above, the multiple small waterfalls spilling from various crevices and splashing into the pool. But the water was too warm and plentiful to be fed from such small streams. I dipped my head back, letting the fresh water from the underground spring wash over my face.

Then arms grasped me from behind as Kensie tried to climb onto my back.

I went under from her sudden weight then bobbed back up by kicking my feet. "I thought you would be glad to be washed clean of the alien sneeze."

"I would be, if I could swim."

CHAPTER TEN

The skyship shuddered as it locked onto the hull of the other Xulonian ship. Kalesh Naz shifted from one foot to the other, as he waited for the docking sequence to be completed.

"You did it." Tyrria squeezed his hand as she stood beside him. "You escaped from the battle moon, and you're reuniting with your Taori brothers."

The kalesh grunted. He had escaped from the Xulonian battle moon—and taken Tyrria with him, like he'd promised—but he was still far from realizing his goal of a reunited crew that was safely back in its own time and space. Only when all Taori warriors were far from the cruel Xulonians and their twisted pleasure moons would he be able to consider his promise fulfilled. "I did not rescue Kaos."

Tyrria readjusted her smaller hand in his. "You couldn't have known that when we took off. You saw him and Kensie on the ship." She bit the corner of her lower lip. "*I* saw them on the ship."

"Yet somehow they did not make it off the moon." Naz's

scowl deepened. "As soon as we regroup with the others and discuss our plans, I will return to the battle moon to retrieve them."

Tyrria peered up at him, her sideswept pink bangs revealing her silver eyes. "Not alone, you won't."

The Taori cut his gaze to her before returning it to the ships docking, the steel hulls groaning as they clamped onto each other and created an airtight seal between the ships. "I won't take you back there. It's too dangerous."

Tyrria looked away from him and faced forward. "That's not really your call, is it?"

He swung his head to her, and his long hair fell over his shoulders. "You are my mate."

"But I'm not one of your Taori warriors. I'm not one of the Ten Thousand you can order around." Her lips quirked as she added. "At least, when we're not in bed."

Naz's eyes widened and he glanced around them, but none of the other females they'd rescued from the battle arena were near them. They were all resting, or recovering from the chaotic rescue, and dealing with the news that their friend and fellow arena attendant had been inadvertently left behind on the moon.

He fought back a grin and cleared his throat, both pleased and vexed that the female he'd given his heart to was so willful. "I am responsible for keeping you safe." His voice devolved to a rasp as his heart squeezed. "I just got you away from there. I cannot risk taking you back."

Tyrria sighed, turning her body so she could take both of his rough, calloused hands in hers. "Loving someone doesn't mean controlling them. I got enough control from my father and the guards in the arena, thank you very much. If we're going to work, you have to trust me."

He met her gaze, holding it with his vivid-blue eyes that

glistened as he gripped her hands tightly. "I do trust you. It's the other aliens I do not trust. It is too dangerous for you to join the rescue for Kaos and Kensie. If I lost you..." His voice cracked and he pressed his lips together until they were a white line.

Tyrria's eyes filled with tears at the sight of the massive, horned warrior allowing himself to display anything but brute strength. "Did you forget that I'm half Lycithian and can shift at will now? I can morph into any type of beast and bite off the heads of any of those guards who attempt to stand in our way." She winked at him. "I'll probably be the one saving your cute ass."

The kalesh choked out a laugh. "You're probably right."

Tyrria dropped one of his hands, and they both pivoted back to face the large airlock that was creaking open.

"So, it's settled," Tyrria said. "I'll come with you to rescue Kaos and Kensie."

Naz grunted his tacit agreement. "More importantly, you think my ass is cute?"

Tyrria's mouth fell open and a laugh spilled out. "That was your takeaway?" She leaned back to and pretended to eye his ass thoughtfully. "Pretty cute, but I do have a particular fondness for your tail."

The tip of the Taori's tail twitched, and a purr of a growl rumbled his chest. Before he could respond, the airlock opened all the way, and a trio of Taori warriors rushed forward.

"Torst! Skard!" Naz forgot any formality associated with his position as ship's kalesh as he threw his arms around the warriors he'd spent most of his life with and who he'd feared he'd never see again. He stared in shock when he realized the third warrior hurrying to greet him. "Daiken! When last I saw you, you were nearly mad with fever."

The Taori pilot's smile was wide as he allowed himself to

be pulled into a hug with all four warriors. "It's a long story, but I am cured of the Quaibyn."

"As are Skard and I," Torst added, eying Naz. "Did the temporal shift provoke the onset of the fever in you, Kalesh?"

Naz gave a curt nod. "It did, but I am also free of the grip of the fever."

Questioning looks were exchanged, and then the three Taori caught sight of Tyrria.

Naz pulled himself to his full height and reached for her hand. "This is Tyrria, my mate."

Skard gave her a small bow, the bone pendant around his neck swinging forward. "It is an honor to meet the female who managed to convince our kalesh there is anything worth pursuing but duty to the mission."

Tyrria's cheeks flushed, as she gazed up at Naz. "I had to maul a few aliens in the process, but he was worth it."

Skard opened and closed his mouth, clearly not sure how to respond to the unusual statement from the delicate-looking female.

Torst barked out a laugh. "Are you sure you aren't part Taori?"

"She is part Lycithian shape-shifter," Naz said. "And very deadly."

Tyrria gave an innocent shrug and smiled brightly at them.

"Then I am glad you're on our side," Daiken said.

"I remember you!" Carly strode onto the ship from the connecting airlock, her gaze locked onto Tyrria. "You were on our transport."

Tyrria sized up the tall woman, her eyes flashing recognition. "And you were security."

"So was Lia." Carly jerked a thumb behind her, as a smaller woman with long, dark hair joined them, and slipped her hand into Torst's.

"Nice to see that the ducking Xulonians didn't kill you," she said to Tyrria.

Tyrria furrowed her brow at the odd word 'ducking.'

"She'll blow an enemy soldier's head off, but she won't curse." Carly shook her head. "I don't fucking get it."

Lia shot Carly a mock scowl that morphed into a grin. "I'm just glad so many of us survived and are back together. One of the scientists from the transport is here with us, too, but you might not have known Val. The scientists kept to themselves on our transport." Lia tossed a glance over her shoulder. "She's busy working on a way to get the Taori back to their own time, otherwise I'm sure she'd be here to say hi."

Naz jerked, his gaze going quickly from one Taori to the other. "There is a possibility of us returning to our own time?"

Daiken nodded. "My mate, I mean, Valeria, is working on the temporal mechanics of returning a ship through the wormhole."

"And we're all going with them," Carly added, as Skard slipped a hand around her waist. "These guys will need some help, if the Sythian swarm is as vicious as they say."

Tyrria tipped her head back to meet Naz's gaze. "I'd follow the kalesh to any time or space, so I'm in."

Naz pulled her close to him, growling and curling his tail around her legs. "First, we need to go back to the battle moon and rescue my first officer."

"Kaos didn't escape with you?" Torst asked, his hand going to the hilt of his blade as if by instinct.

The kalesh gave a curt shake of his head. "I will return to the moon to retrieve him while you all work on our plan to find the other Taori scattered throughout the Xulonian system and bring down the aliens who destroyed our ship."

Tyrria elbowed him gently in the ribs. "With me."

Naz released a guttural sound and then a tortured sigh. "With my mate by my side."

"We're not letting you go alone." Torst scanned the other Taori, who shook their head in unison. "We're going with you."

Naz frowned. "You're disobeying an order from your kalesh?"

Skard stepped forward and clamped a hand on the Taori's shoulder. "There are other Taori who can work on our plan to destroy the Xulonian. You need your officers by your side. Kaos is our first officer, too."

Naz furrowed his brow. "Other Taori?"

Daiken braced his hands on his hips. "While you've been fighting in the arena, Torst has been locating the other escape pods and rescuing our crew mates."

Torst gave a half shrug. "We will need to acquire a bigger ship. It's getting a little cramped in the one we have."

Naz shook his head in amazement. "I said we would rejoin even stronger than before. It looks like I was right. Our fate was written in the stars." He squared his shoulders. "Into the valley of death ride the Ten Thousand."

"We are the Taori," his warriors chanted with him. "We are the Immortals."

Before Naz could feel too flush with the impending victory, a creature with shaggy, pale hair popped his head through from the other ship. "If you're done with your war chants, we're being hailed by an unknown ship."

CHAPTER ELEVEN

Kensie

I spat out a mouthful of water as Kaos hoisted me onto a flat rock rising slightly above the pool. What was left of my clothing clung to me like a second skin, and was nearly transparent. The only upside to being drenched was that I was no longer encrusted with sand or mucus.

"How do you not swim?" The Taori heaved himself onto the rock beside me and flopped onto his back. His voice echoed off the rocks that rose high around us and was amplified by the water.

I shrugged and rolled so that I was on my back looking up, as well. "The planet I grew up on didn't have any large bodies of water, so it wasn't much of a priority. Then I ended up here, and the biggest pool was the bathing pools in the winner suites. You don't need to know how to swim to use one of those."

He released a breath and a grunt that told me he still questioned my lack of swimming ability. "I never saw the winner suites."

"If you'd stayed long enough to fight, I'm sure you would have."

"Not if they'd made me fight against my kalesh."

I twisted my head to look at him. His hair was even darker now that it was wet, and droplets of water clung to his horns, making the silvery stripes glisten. "Because you think he would have beaten you?"

"Because I would never have raised a hand against my kalesh."

I rolled my head back, so I was peering at the sliver of white sky peeking between the towering sides of the canyon. "You Taori do seem to take the honor and duty thing pretty seriously."

"Honor is all there is."

He said this with such certainty that I remained silent. Being forced to take part in the Xulonians' bloodlust had numbed me to loftier ideals. Honor was hard to value when survival and not being punished by your shock collar were your only goals.

"How did you learn to swim? I thought you'd been living on a spaceship for most of your life."

"We have been traveling by sky ship for longer than a human lifetime, but that means that we've stopped on many planets to resupply and refuel. Some of those planets contained seas or vast lakes. It seemed wise to learn how to swim so we could experience these environments."

The planet where I'd been raised had been almost as arid and featureless as the moon we were stranded on, and it was hard to imagine large bodies of water. "I've never even seen a sea or lake."

Kaos propped himself on his elbows, letting his gaze drift to the pool hidden within the cavern. "Imagine this pool with no end that your eyes can detect, and a floor so deep you can never reach it."

I shivered at the thought, a slight breeze cooling the drops of water on my skin. It had been frightening enough flailing in the small pool. I couldn't imagine something so vast. "No thanks. I've had my fill of swimming for a while."

"You did not swim. I dragged you across the pool while you flapped your arms and kicked like the water was assaulting you."

My cheeks warmed at his description of me. "That's what swimming looks like."

He swiveled his head to me and cocked one eyebrow. "I assure you, it does not."

I muttered something in my defense about watching historical vids about swimming, but he'd already stood and was clearly not listening to me.

"Now that we've found a place to shelter, we need food."

I wasn't sure if I'd say we found shelter. More like we'd fallen headfirst into it. But he was right about food. My stomach rumbled at the mention of it, and it occurred to me that I hadn't eaten a bite since we'd left the arena complex. Since he'd come from the dungeons, he might not have eaten for even longer.

I scanned the contained area with the pool. Aside from striated rock jutting into the sky, there weren't any signs of vegetation and there certainly were no animals. "Where?"

Kaos nodded to the pool. "We can start by drinking the fresh water."

I licked my lips where some droplets remained. He was right. It was drinkable. I'd heard of seawater being salty, but this didn't have any salty tang.

"If the water is sweet and fed by underground springs, then there are probably plants and creatures within it."

I scuttled back from the edge. "Creatures? Like the one we ended up inside?"

He eyed me, his lips twitching. "I doubt it. This pool is much too small to support large marine life. Besides, if there was a massive water creature, I'm sure it would have tried to eat us already."

"Very comforting," I mumbled and ignored the merriment dancing in the Taori's incredibly blue eyes.

He stepped closer to the edge of the rock and peered over. "The bottom does not look to be too far down."

I craned my neck without moving closer, but I couldn't get a full view. If Kaos was hoping I'd join him in exploring the unknown depths of the spring, he was out of luck. "You don't think there are fish, do you?"

He shrugged. "There is only one way to know." Then without another word, he peeled off the dark pants that hung wet to his legs and stepped out of them.

I didn't bother to mask my shock as the Taori stood completely naked beside me. Not only did the dark ink covering his chest extend down his torso and legs, but his long tail sprouted from his body right above a perfect, round ass, which was one of the only parts of him not marked. I'd seen my fair share of naked aliens in my time as an attendant to the arena fighters, but I'd never seen a male with such a long, thick cock or one with three broad crowns down the length of it. Either the aliens had had some other kind of reproductive organ—like the part-amphibian alien who had two tentacles dangling between its legs, or the furry beast whose cock was embedded in its body, and it slowly extended like an accordion straw—or they hadn't been nearly as well endowed. I tried to swallow but my throat was as bone dry as the desert.

As quickly and wordlessly as he'd disrobed, the Taori dove into the turquoise water and sent drops splashing onto my legs. I scooted to the edge, forgetting my previous jitters about the water and fears of something living within it. Watching Kaos leap into the water had been enough to leave me breathless. I couldn't resist watching him cut through the water, his naked body moving so gracefully I wondered if the Taori evolved from fish.

I held my breath as his huge body delved deep, but the water was so clear I didn't lose track of him as he touched the bottom and then swam in a wide circle before shooting up and emerging with one hand high.

"Moss!" He said it as if it was a wonderful thing.

He kicked over and handed it to me.

The spongy handful of green dripped through my fingers, but I managed a grin. "Yum."

He dove again. His tail flipped through the air followed by his ass, and I almost dropped the handful of moss as my gaze tracked him. Through the diffusion of the water, I couldn't tell for a moment if it was his long cock trailing as he twisted under the water or his tail.

My pulse fluttered and my heart hammered wildly in my chest as all the heat in my body pooled between my legs. I sat back and let the moss drop onto the rock with a splat. Either I was experiencing heat stroke, or I was in serious trouble.

"Please let it be heat stroke," I whispered furtively to myself.

CHAPTER TWELVE

Kaos

The water wasn't cold but compared to the scorching sun of the desert and my feverish skin, it felt cool as I dove down to the bottom again. I closed my eyes for a beat to savor the rush of water over my legs as I scissored them, my tail drifting in the current they created.

Opening my eyes, I spotted another clump of green clinging to a stone, and I wedged my fingers under it to pry it off. It wouldn't be the best thing I'd ever eaten but at least it would provide nutrients. And it could be no worse than Zenghay slugs, which were eaten live and wiggling.

My chest burned as I flipped over and kicked off the bottom, shooting to the surface as my lungs ached for air. I was out of practice holding my breath underwater, so I was lucky the pool wasn't deep.

I burst out of the water, sucking in the warm air and

kicking over to where Kensie sat. I handed her the clump of moss and hung onto the stone as I trod water.

She didn't meet my gaze as she took the moss and shook it, sending droplets scattering. Then busied herself by spreading it out on the stone. "I thought it might be better dried."

I flattened both palms on the ledge and heaved myself from the pool, twisting and landing on my ass with my legs hanging over the edge. "It's too bad you don't swim. The water feels nice."

"I remember it." She pointed to the rock overhang we'd slid down. "I did fall in with you."

I eyed her, curious that she was taking great pains not to look at me. Was she upset about what I'd done when we were inside the tunnels we now knew were the insides of a sand creature? I'd explained the Quaibyn, but maybe she didn't believe me, or maybe she still held a grudge that I'd taken her from the arena in the first place.

I stood and stepped a few steps away before I shook myself, sending more water flying, then I ran both hands through my hair to squeeze out the excess water, and finally, I wrung out the tip of my tail. I scooped up the pants I'd left in a heap and shook them out before spreading them out to dry on the flattest rock I could find.

Then I returned to where the female was worrying over the moss. Her dress had been torn and dirty when we'd fallen into the tunnels, but now it was merely shreds of sheer fabric that was adhered to her skin while being almost entirely transparent.

"You should take that off."

She snapped her head up, her cheeks flaming pink. "What?"

"Your clothes are wet. You can't be comfortable." I took a

step toward her. “I can dry what’s left of your dress alongside my pants.”

She opened and closed her mouth, doing an impressive impersonation of a Grendellen puffer fish, before shaking her head and standing quickly. “It’s not that wet.”

I glanced at the water dripping from her, and tried not to notice that her pebbled nipples were on full display and a solid indicator that she was chilled. “You’re standing in a puddle.”

She dropped her gaze to the ground and the small pool forming around her feet before glancing back up just as fast. “I don’t mind letting it dry while I wear it.”

She nibbled on her bottom lip as her gaze darted to me, sliding down my body and up as the color in her cheeks deepened.

Was she disturbed by my nakedness? I tried to remember what I knew of humans, but I’d picked up nothing about their modesty levels. But hadn’t she been assigned to bathe and attend to alien fighters in the arena? Surely she’d seen plenty of naked males.

“Does it bother you that I’m not wearing clothes?”

She kept her gaze locked on mine. “Not really.”

“You weren’t exposed to naked males when you worked in the arena?”

She put her hands on her hips. “I was, but none of them were so...” She flapped a hand in the direction of my cock. “You know...enormous, not to mention your three....” She clamped her mouth shut, as if she couldn’t believe she’d uttered those words.

Her admission startled me, and the words made my heart pound and my cock almost instantly thicken. If she’d been startled by my size before, this was not going to help matters.

Kensie sucked in a breath as my cock hardened and started to rise. “Holy...” Her eyes widened and she slapped a hand over her mouth to stop herself from saying whatever it was she was going to say.

I crossed my arms over myself in an attempt to salvage the situation. “Taori are accustomed to nudity, so I forget that not all species are as comfortable with it. As soon as my pants are dry—“

My words died on my lips as I watched her take another step back and into nothing but air. Her mouth formed a perfect circle before she pinwheeled her arms as she tried in vain to regain her balance before she plunged backward into the water. With a curse, I lunged for her, catching her around the waist as we fell together.

For the second time, we were submerged in the pool. This time we bobbed to the surface quicker, with Kenzie’s arms wrapped around my neck as she faced me. She gasped and wrapped her legs around my waist, as I treaded water to keep us both afloat.

Our faces were so close that her rapid breath mingled with mine. Her pupils were wide as her chest heaved, her hard nipples pressed into my skin. The cool water hadn’t been enough to soften my cock, and her ass bounced on the hard bar of it as I kicked.

Before I could apologize, or swim us to the side, she let out a small moan and crushed her lips to mine.

CHAPTER
THIRTEEN

Kensie

The softness of his lips was almost as much of a shock as the fact that I was kissing the Taori at all. Had I been the one to kiss him? I barely knew as I allowed myself to sink into the kiss, my fingers winding into his wet hair. My heart thudded as his hand slipped to the back of my head, his broad palm holding my face to his as his fingers tangled in my hair.

Even if I'd started it, Kaos was the one who deepened the kiss, opening my lips to him and caressing my tongue with his. I moaned into his mouth as I slid my hands up until I'd reached his horns. My fingertips feathered across the raised ridges that striped the hard curves, and I made fists around them, squeezing hard.

The growl that arose within him made me jump and tear my lips from his. I pulled back to see that his eyes were nearly black pools of molten desire, and his jaw was tight, with a muscle pulsing in his neck.

"Did I hurt you?" I asked, my mind still muddled from the rush of the kiss.

"No, but if you continue to touch my horns, I will not be able to control my Quaibyn."

For a moment, I thought he'd named his cock Quaibyn, then I remembered that was the name for his mating fever. My gaze went to his silvery-striped horns, and I quickly uncurled my fingers. "Your horns are sensitive?"

He murmured a low, gravelly sound. "Mmmmm. Every Taori experiences the Quaibyn differently. Some lose all awareness and memory of their actions, some gain incredible strength, and some have heightened senses. I become highly sensitive. When I am in the full throes of the fever, the slightest breeze across my skin is like an embrace, and I can hear a blade of grass snap across a savannah."

"So, your horns aren't normally sensitive?" My hands were still touching his horns although I no longer squeezed them.

"They are. A Taori's horns are one of his erogenous zones, but when I am experiencing the fever, touching them can bring me to the edge as if you were wrapping your pretty little fingers around my—"

"Oh!" I jerked back my hands as if his horns were hot pokers. "I'm so sorry."

The corner of his mouth quivered, and he shifted his hand in my hair. "You have no reason to be sorry. I enjoyed every moment of it." He pulled my head as if to kiss me again, but I leaned back.

I didn't know why exactly I'd kissed him, but I knew better than to screw a guy I just met and who very well might die. As hot as he was and as much as I wanted to know what it would be like to bring him to climax by stroking his horns—not to mention what I wanted to know about his huge cock with three heads—I couldn't get attached to someone I might lose again.

"I don't think we should, I mean, I know I kissed you, at least I think I did, but I shouldn't have done that." The words spilled from me in a jumble, and I let my gaze drop from his face. "We're trying to escape from this place and the last thing either of us need is more complications."

He grunted, the hold on my head loosening as he slid his hand from my hair to my back.

I snuck a look at him, but if I was expecting to see disappointment or hurt on his face, I was wrong. The heat in his eyes had cooled and his expression had hardened, even though the muscle still ticked in his jaw.

"You are right."

I felt the need to apologize again but my throat tightened, and the words wouldn't come out. What kind of game was I playing? I was the one to impulsively kiss him—and it hadn't been just an innocent peck, either—then I tried to be the voice of reason, as if I wasn't the one who'd thrown caution to the wind. My face was hot as I thought of stroking his horns before I'd known just what that did to him. If I really meant what I said about not wanting complications, why did I desperately want to touch his horns again, and hear the desperate, dark growl that rumbled up from his chest?

"Hold on to me," Kaos said, as he used one arm to pull us both through the water toward the rock ledge.

Embarrassment flamed my cheeks as I had to let him swim me to the side. If I'd been worried that things weren't awkward enough after he'd scented me when we'd been inside the sand creature and then disrobed completely, I'd taken care of that. Now it would be truly uncomfortable to be around each other.

Good going, Kensie.

I didn't usually act first and think later, but it had been a long day, and all my usual barriers and walls to keep me from getting attached didn't seem to be working like they usually did. I'd gotten pretty good at detaching emotionally after watching fighter after fighter be killed in the battle ring. After allowing myself to fall for one and getting my heart broken, I'd promised myself I would never let myself feel anything again for someone who could be taken from me. And since we were stranded on a hostile moon that was only inhabited by aliens who wanted to enslave or kill us—or creatures who want to eat us—that definitely included Kaos.

Then why did I feel such a powerful pull to him? Why did it feel like he wasn't a stranger? And why, when he'd told me he was suffering from a mating fever that made it almost impossible for him to control his lust, did I not really want him to control it? Part of me wanted to help him cure his fever and use me in whatever way he needed to slake his carnal hunger. This stark realization made my heart catch in my chest.

I glanced at the Taori as he reached the edge and slapped one hand on the stone. I was being an idiot to even consider helping the Taori cure his fever. The alien wasn't even from my time. He was the absolute last guy I should fall for, or even contemplate being more than friendly partners in escape. He was trying to return to his own time and space, not hook up with a human who was more a liability than anything. Once we were rescued, we would go our separate ways. End of story.

I shivered as it hit me that I was hardly who he'd have chosen to be trapped with on an alien moon. It hadn't been him who'd kissed me. He'd even stopped me when I'd practically molested his horns. Who was the one who couldn't control their urges now?

I accepted his help in crawling back onto the rock and politely looked away as he hoisted up his naked body.

"There is something I need from you," he said, once we were sitting side by side.

My pulse jackknifed, and I practically whispered, "What?"

"If you're going to continue to fall into the water, I insist that you let me teach you to swim."

CHAPTER
FOURTEEN

Kensie

"This is almost as bad as eating that green mush." I made a face, as Kaos treaded water in the middle of the pool and attempted to coax me from the wall.

"The moss had nutrients." He gave me a severe look, although I doubt he disagreed with me about the flavor and texture of our meager meal. It had been both mushy and slightly bitter, and even he'd grimaced as he'd swallowed it down.

"That's all it had," I grumbled as I hung from the ledge with one hand, the tips of my fingers white as they grasped the rough stone.

"My swimming instruction is as torturous as the green mush?"

I huffed out a reluctant breath. "It's not your teaching. I just don't think I'm very good at it." I eyed the greenish-blue water I was partially suspended in, as if it were a vat of poison. "Maybe humans aren't meant to swim."

He rolled his eyes as he stretched his long arms to the side. "You weigh as much as a Velleren water bug. If I can swim, you can swim."

I glared at him, taking great care not to let my gaze drift beneath the water, since his pants were still drying. "Are all Taori as patient as you are?"

"They are less so. Taori learn to swim by being thrown into deep water."

I inhaled quickly, the thought of being tossed in and forced to literally sink or swim giving me a sliver of appreciation for the alien who was kicking in the middle of the pool to keep himself afloat as he waited for me to release the wall and put the skills he'd taught me to practice.

"If I drown, it's on your conscience," I said under my breath, as I finally let go of the rock and started to kick madly under the water. My mind raced as I tried to remember the instruction he'd given me about moving my hands through the water to propel myself forward, but my body started to sink. I closed my eyes as my head went under, reaching forward with my cupped hands and pulling them toward me. Then my head was breaking the surface, and I was moving closer to him. I repeated my movements, my arms cutting through the water as I kicked behind me. I was swimming.

"I'm doing it!" I cried, opening my mouth and immediately sucking down a large gulp of water.

I started to choke and sink again, but this time strong arms circled my waist and held me up.

"Not bad," Kaos said. "You almost made it to me."

"You didn't have to grab me," I said, hacking up the last remnants of water. "I could have made it."

"I didn't want your drowning on my conscience," he said as

he released his tight hold on me. "But now you can kick to keep yourself up."

Panic flared as I started to sink but I scissored my legs vigorously under me, and my head rose again. "This would be easier if I wasn't starving."

He grunted, his mouth pulling down. "You are right. We won't be able to last forever on moss."

"Forever? Who said anything about forever? We only have to last until your friend comes back for us."

Kaos took one of my hands and led me back to the side. "My kalesh will come for us, but I need to find a way to alert him to our location. We are well hidden from the alien guards and protected from sand creatures, but our hiding spot might make it difficult for us to be found."

I nibbled on my bottom lip. As much as I wanted to be found and rescued, it was hard for me to think of what would come next. I had no idea how long I'd been on the Xulonian moon and working in their arena complex, but it was long enough that I'd almost forgotten what it was like to live in a normal society. I'd been little more than a teenager when I'd been abducted and brought to the battle moon. What would my life be outside this world? What would I do without any family or job? I doubted there was much call for tending to wounded, alien gladiators in the empire.

"Kensie?"

I looked over to where Kaos was already sitting on the side, holding out a hand to me. "Right." I grasped his hand and let him heave me out as water sluiced down my body and my drenched dress. "We can't stay here forever." I forced a laugh. "Especially with our current cuisine."

"At least I can leave you here to search for more food and a way to signal our presence without worrying that you'll stumble into the water and drown."

I made a face at him. "You act like I spontaneously rolled into the pool."

He lifted one brow and twitched a single shoulder. I refused to admit that I'd backed into the water because I was so freaked out by the sight of him naked. Not when I was trying to convince him that I wasn't completely helpless.

"I'll be fine. I *have* survived on this moon for a long time, even if it was in the arena. Not every woman who was brought to the battle arena as an attendant lasted."

His gaze went to my neck where I used to wear a metal ring that was electrified and used by the guards to keep the females in line. "You are right. I do not know what it is like to be under another's control." He met my eyes, his blue ones intense. "You will never be anyone's captive again, I promise you."

I wanted to tell him not to make promises he couldn't keep. The fighter I'd loved had promised that he would continue to win, but it hadn't been a vow the Xulonians would have ever allowed him to keep. The one valuable thing the cruel aliens had taught me was not to believe empty words and promises made in the heat of passion.

As much as I wanted to hang onto Kaos' words and let them fill me with comfort, they were as fleeting as the wind and the sun. He couldn't assure me that the guards wouldn't find us before his kalesh, even though I know he believed what he was saying with every fiber of his being.

I smiled at him. Maybe my doubts didn't matter. Maybe all that counted was how much he believed that we would be rescued. I didn't mind borrowing some of his hope, if it meant I could have half of his confidence.

"I promise you that I'll be here when you get back." I slapped my palm on the rock. "Safely on dry land."

CHAPTER FIFTEEN

Kaos

My pants were stiff as I took long strides up the sloped rock, and my cock rubbed against the rigid leather. If it had been my choice, I would have left them behind, but the female seemed completely flustered by my lack of clothing. Or, as she'd put it, the distraction of my enormous cock.

My fingers twitched, and my cock strained inside my uncomfortably tight pants, as my mind wandered back to holding Kensie in my arms in the water and running my hand through her hair. When I remembered the feel of her lips on mine as she'd startled me with the kiss, I groaned aloud, the deep sound echoing off the looming stone as I wound my way through a tight passageway. She'd tasted so sweet, and her lips had been yielding and soft beneath mine. It was impossible not to imagine the rest of her body yielding to me, her legs falling open and her… I gave my head a rough shake, trying to dislodge the images that threatened to make my cock burst from my pants

"Focus," I said to myself, my voice as strained as my tenuous grasp on control.

I needed to stay sharp as I navigated through the peaks, or I might not find Kensie again. We'd found the spring-fed pool by accident, and I couldn't count on losing my way and stumbling upon it again. Or, falling down a steep, rock slide into it.

I took a few deep breaths to steady myself even though my hands tingled with heat and my flesh burned. If I'd hoped being away from Kensie would help subdue my approaching fever, thinking about her hadn't helped. Still, I narrowed my gaze on my surroundings and tried to memorize the path I was taking to the summit.

The best way to send a signal would be to get as high as possible. Kalesh Naz would know me and my training well enough that he would search for me at a high point. Now I needed to get there and manage to configure a way to signal him.

Despite being stranded on the alien moon with a human with few, if any, survival skills, I hadn't lost faith that we would be rescued. Even when he was locked in the battle arena and forced to fight for his life, my kalesh hadn't given up his goal of escaping and reuniting our crew. He'd never wavered in his mission, and as his first officer, I would never falter in mine. Being stranded with Kensie was merely a bump in the journey.

I bent my head to duck under a low slab of brown rock and flattened my back to edge along a narrow ledge. At least the human was safe. I'd done my duty as an honorable Taori by protecting her, even though what I truly wanted to do was tear the flimsy wisps of fabric from her flesh and claim her body for myself.

At once, my feet slipped, and a few pebbles skittered down the deep crevice. I sucked in a breath and regained my balance, pressing my back against the rock and evening my breath. Even if I didn't die protecting her from the alien guards, I was going to die because I was so distracted by the thought of her.

"There's no point." She might have kissed me, but as soon as I told her about my horns and how the Quaibyn affected me, she'd retreated. She didn't want any complications, and my raging mating fever was a significant complication since the only way to cure it was by mating and securing a female in the mating lock. I was sure that being bound to me by the swollen crown at the base of my cock would fall squarely into the category of a complication.

It didn't matter. Kalesh Naz would come for us before my fever became an issue. Even as I told myself this, the words felt like a lie. Already, my horns buzzed with acute sensitivity, and my ears pricked as I detected more distant sounds.

I reached the end of the ledge, exhaling as I found footing on a wider ledge. Then I tilted my head. The sounds were of water, but it wasn't the water that trickled into the pool where I'd left Kenzie. That was behind me, and these noises came from someplace ahead of me.

I picked up my pace, curious if there was another spring-fed pool tucked within the rocks. It made sense that the planet would have water sources if there was life beneath the sands—even if there wasn't much life—but the presence of so much water was a surprise.

I was careful to count the turns I made as I followed the sound. Left, right, right, then straight down a slick path that felt like a ramp. I leaned back to slow my pace, not wanting to slip and fall down another slide and into a pool. My pants were barely dry from my first unplanned swim.

When I rounded a sharp bend, I stopped short. The pool

nestled under a low overhang was significantly smaller than the first one, but the water appeared to be bubbling. I crouched down and dipped my hand in, sighing at the heat that enveloped my fingers. It reminded me of the hot pools on Kerros III that were known for their healing properties and drew visitors from all over. I'd spent a pleasant afternoon in one of those pools with my fellow Taori officers while we stopped to refuel.

I briefly considered stripping off my pants and soaking in the heat, but then I reminded myself of my current mission. I needed to reach the pinnacle before darkness fell, and already the light was fading from the sky. I had few recollections from my time alone on the desert before I'd been captured by the alien guards, but I did remember that the moon became frigid once the sun had vanished from the sky. I'd gone from running from the scorching heat to fearing I would freeze to death.

I made a mental note of the location of the steaming water as I stood. I might not have the need to warm up since my skin was prickling with feverish heat, but Kensie wasn't consumed by a raging fever. If she got cold, I might need some way to warm her that didn't involve my body heat.

Pushing aside thoughts of the human and the many ways I could warm her using my body, I retraced my steps and continued up the rocky range. Now that dusk was stealing over the jagged ridges, there were new sounds—chirping, scuttling, and cawing. The desert wasn't the only place on the moon inhabited by alien creatures, although I hoped these were smaller than the animal we'd been inside.

I welcomed the cool night air as it settled over my skin and brought respite from the pulsing heat. I gulped down greedy lungfuls and let it suffuse my bones. Maybe I could control this bout of the Quaibyn, after all. Rescue was imminent, and if I could wait out the scorching heat of the moon's days and avoid thinking about Kensie, the nights would cool me off and allow me to regain control. Already, my mind felt calmer, and my heart slowed to its normal pace.

I trudged up and up, winding higher and squeezing myself through narrow gaps until I emerged at what appeared to be the top of the highest peak. There was a flat area large enough for two people at most with a large, sloping bounder on one side. I rested my back on the boulder as I caught my breath.

From high, the surface of the alien moon seemed even more desolate. I twisted my head in all directions, but the only sign of habitation was the domed complex that glittered in the distance. The sparkling arena and the attached complex with its colorful glass domes looked like twinkling jewels scattered on the sand, but I knew the cruelty and bloodlust that lay beneath the opulence.

At least many of the captive females were now free, but I wished that we could have liberated every fighter in the complex and killed all the guards. The only way to ensure that the arena wasn't resupplied with alien gladiators and abducted females to attend them was to destroy the entire complex. I loosed a satisfied growl at the thought of the buildings exploding and fire dancing across the desert as the Xulonian creation was destroyed.

That could only happen if the Taori were able to secure a ship—preferably a fleet of ships—and enough allies to wage war against the Xulonian criminals. I tipped my head back to peer at the sky, marveling at the vast number of stars twinkling against the velvety blackness. Somewhere up there, Kalesh Naz was planning a rescue—if he wasn't already on his way. I knew this just as surely as I knew that my fate was etched in the fabric of the sky that now stretched above me.

I let my gaze fall back to the desert, which was now dark and empty, although I was all too aware of what dwelled beneath the sandy surface. Then my breath hitched in my throat when I spotted the caravan of lights moving ever closer to the rocky ridges where Kensie and I had found refuge. Was the procession of lights Kalesh Naz leading a rescue or the alien guards on the hunt? Then a strange diffraction at the base of the rocky range and a significant divot in the sand—as if something massive and heavy was compressing it—made my stomach lurch.

CHAPTER SIXTEEN

Kensie

I yawned, not bothering to stifle the sound that echoed back to me off the towering rock. The light that peeked in from the narrow crevice at the top had already faded, and I suspected that I'd soon be sitting alone in the dark.

Glancing around, I told myself that I wasn't afraid of the dark or being alone. Besides, I wasn't alone. Kaos was somewhere nearby and would be returning soon. At least there didn't seem to be enormous beasts like the one we'd actually been inside under the sand. I swiveled my head to take in the placid surface of the water and the quiet stone walls. No, I was almost certain I was the only creature near the pool, which was just fine by me.

I leaned back, bracing myself on my palms, and I tipped my head to eye the sliver of sky that was morphing from colorless to dusky gray. It had been so long since I'd been able to look up at the sky that I felt like I could happily stare at it for ages. Despite the battle arena complex being filled with light, the glass was all colored or mottled, so it had been impossible to get a glimpse of the outside.

I wondered if Kaos was getting a better view of the sky as he ventured higher into the mountains. Unease stirred in my belly, but I brushed it aside. The Taori was tough and clever. There was no need to worry about him. Besides, the range of rocky peaks hadn't proven to be particularly perilous, unless you couldn't swim.

"Which I can," I said with a certain amount of pride. I might not be winning any races anytime soon, but I could keep myself afloat and make it from one side of the pool to the other.

I eyed the water before remembering the promise I'd made to Kaos. I wouldn't go into the water until he returned. Not that I was eager to get my clothes wet again. The gossamer fabric of my dress had just dried, and I didn't know how much more abuse it could take before falling to pieces. That promise would be easy to keep.

I thought about the promises he'd made me. Kaos had vowed that he'd get me off the planet, and make sure I was never anyone's captive again. Considering that we were currently on the alien moon and the only other inhabitants were the arena guards and Xulonians, I hoped, rather than believed, Kaos could keep his promises.

A wave of exhaustion passed through me as I thought about everything that had happened to us since we'd attempted to escape from the battle moon. It was hard to believe it had only been one very long day, but the days on the moon did seem to stretch out unusually long. I lay back with my hands laced behind my head and let my heavy eyelids droop.

I hadn't made any promise to Kaos about staying awake until he returned. Besides, I had no clue how long it might take him to reach a high point in the mountains. He could be winding up through the rocks all night.

Another yawn made my eyes water. I exhaled loudly and closed my eyes, promising myself I would only rest them for a little while. The gentle sounds of the water spilling into the pool from above mingled with faint, emerging chirps, lulling me deeper to sleep.

Then an unfamiliar sound made my body jerk awake. I opened my eyes but didn't move from my prone position on my back. The noise had been soft, but that was what had alerted me. It had sounded purposefully quiet, as if someone was trying to mask their movements.

I remained motionless as I held my breath, waiting for another sound. The water continued to lightly splash, and the desert insects made rhythmic chirping sounds, but there was nothing else. I'd almost convinced myself I'd imagined it and closed my eyes again when I heard it.

Shudders wracked my body. Someone was nearby, and if I wasn't mistaken, they were watching me. My pulse jangled as I tried to detect movement from my peripheral vision, but whoever was hiding was good at it. There wasn't even a shadow dancing from behind a slab of rock.

Then I almost laughed. Kaos. Who else could it be? He'd returned from his mission to the top and was spying on me, either to make sure I wasn't playing around in the water, or because he had a secret voyeuristic streak. If it was the arena guards, they would have rushed forward and captured me. There was nothing subtle or quiet about the thick-necked creatures who did the Xulonians bidding as they lumbered on heavy feet and breathed through prominent tusks. They couldn't sneak up on anyone.

I fought the urge to call out to Kaos and tell him his game was up. Then I had a better idea. I'd pretend I didn't know he was observing me and put on a little show for him. Maybe I'd even pretend I was jumping into the pool to see how fast he jumped in after me. I cut my gaze to my dress that was barely holding onto my shoulders by frayed straps. Or maybe I'd just tease him while I stayed on land.

It might be playing with fire to tease the alien who claimed to be afflicted by mating fever, but I got the sense that he was attracted to me, and not only because of his curse. Let's see if I was right, I thought as I made a production of sitting up and stretching my arms over my head. I arched my back so that my breasts were on full display.

Part of me expected him to rush out, growling at me and scowling like he was furious at me for being female. But nothing happened, and he didn't emerge. Just as I was returning to my reclined pose, I heard another barely audible shift, which told me he was watching.

I should have called out to him, but if he wasn't going to tell me he was watching me then why should I tell him I knew he was there? I scooted myself over to the edge of the flat rock, humming as I let my legs dangle over the water. Then I hoisted the fabric of my dress so that it was bunched up almost to my waist, my legs fully exposed. I figured my proximity to the pool would provoke a response, and if that didn't do it, flashing so much bare flesh just might. But there was nothing.

Finally, I huffed out an impatient breath. "I guess I should get naked and jump in the water. You sure you don't want to join me?"

"That's an unexpected offer, but I'll just watch you." The voice was deep and dangerous—sending ice dancing along my skin—but it wasn't familiar. Neither was the imposing creature with platinum hair and a leather kilt who stepped from behind a rock.

CHAPTER SEVENTEEN

Kaos

I abandoned all thoughts of establishing some sort of beacon to alert Kalesh Naz as I raced back down the steep, winding path. I couldn't explain the panic welling up inside me, but my warrior instincts told me that something was wrong. There wasn't enough light for me to determine what was at the base of the mountains, but there was something massive that wasn't visible to the naked eye.

I cursed as I ducked a sharp overhang and skidded a bit on the hardpacked ground, pebbles skittering over the side and plummeting down. Now I sounded crazy, even to myself. Did I truly believe an invisible monstrosity had tracked us to the rocky range? The alien moon might contain huge sand beasts, but those weren't invisible, even if they did dwell out of sight.

My heart hammered so loudly it drowned out all sounds but my racing thoughts. I was sure I'd seen the sand at the base of the mountains indented significantly, as if something massive was pressing down on it. Massive and invisible.

I gave my head a rough shake. I knew it sounded crazy, but that didn't change the fact that my spine tingled with unease. It wasn't even the Quaibyn, although I suspected my heightened senses might have something to do with my body being on high alert. Even the air felt different now, and I detected the presence of others.

My fingers prickled like they always did before a battle, although I'd never raced headlong into a fight with an opponent I couldn't see. Was this more of the Xulonians' tricks? Did they have the ability to shield themselves from sight? I grunted my disgust at the aliens who'd destroyed my ship, hoping that it was them I was preparing to fight. I wouldn't mind spilling Xulonian blood.

I'd been running on instinct, but I'd managed to make all the right turns, passing the smaller pool and then winding back across a narrow pass and finally closing in on the pool where I'd left Kensie. I slowed as I approached, steadying my breath so I didn't startle her if the danger was all in my head.

When I spotted her, I blew out a breath of relief. She was still there, although I'd expected her to be sleeping or at least relaxing. Instead, she was standing with her shoulders stiff. A quick scan of her body told me she was unharmed and dry, so she'd kept her promise not to go into the water.

She whirled around, her eyes wide. "Kaos."

"So, this is the mate you told me about."

My gaze immediately tracked the voice, and my hand went to my waist where my blade would normally hang. The speaker was an alien approximately my size with hair so pale it was almost white. It hung over his shoulders, which were bare. His only clothing was a skirt made from straps of worn, brown leather that hung halfway down his sizable thighs. A strap crossed his chest and held a shiny battle axe across his back. A few swirls were inked across his chest, and a tail swished behind him.

My tail kept pace with him, slicing through the air as we faced off across from each other. Kensie hurried to my side and slipped her hand into mine.

My gaze never left his as I sized up my opponent. "Who are you?"

"I am Raas Ronnan of the Kyrie Vandar." He said this as if I should know what any of those words meant.

Kensie sucked in a sharp breath, telling me that they did mean something to her.

"Do you know these warriors?" I asked her in a low voice without glancing at her.

"The Vandar are raiders from a couple of sectors over. They're outlaws who fly in invisible hordes of ships. No one wants to encounter a Vandar horde. They'll raid your ship, scavenge everything, and kill anyone who stands in their way."

The Vandar who called himself Raas Ronnan grinned. Even though she'd whispered, he'd clearly picked up what she'd said. "It seems our reputation precedes us, but I'm not the Raas of the hordes you speak of." His smile faltered. "I'm here to exact revenge on those Vandar."

I wasn't sure what he was talking about, but it didn't seem to have much to do with me or Kensie. "What are you doing on this moon?"

"My horde encountered some of your fellow Taori."

My heart seemed to stop for a moment as I stared at him. If the Vandar hordes were as ruthless as Kensie had heard...

"Your crew mates are safe," Ronnan said as if he'd read my mind. "I have no fight with warriors who have also been displaced and abandoned."

I released a breath. "Then why are you on this alien moon? Why is my kalesh not here instead?"

The Vandar inclined his head and gave a half shrug. "Only Vandar warbirds can fly unseen."

So, I had seen an invisible ship at the base of the mountain. "You can fly behind the veil?"

He furrowed his brow. "We have invisibility shielding, which the Xulonian ships your Taori brothers have commandeered, do not have. I offered to find you and return you to them. Kalesh Naz told me to tell you that this was written in the stars and that he looks forward to fighting side by side with his first officer again."

The uneasy feeling that had been roiling in my belly since I'd first spotted the invisible Vandar ship on the desert started to evaporate when I heard the Vandar speak Naz's words. I now believed Raas Ronnan, and I knew in my gut that he'd been sent by my kalesh. This meant that Naz's plan to regroup our crew and defeat the Xulonians was coming to pass. My skin buzzed with the anticipation of raining punishment on the aliens who'd destroyed our sky ship and scattered my Taori brothers.

Ronnan's gaze slid to Kensie. "Along with a female who was also a captive of the Xulonians. They did not mention that you two were mates."

Kensie squeezed my hand, which I took as a silent indication to go along with her lie. "She is right. We are mates."

Raas Ronan lifted one eyebrow as he eyed us. "That is too bad. The female is alluring, and she invited me to swim naked with her in the pool."

Kensie gasped. "That's when I thought you were..." Her words drifted and she shifted from one foot to the next.

The Vandar folded his arms over his chest, amusement flickering in his eyes. "Curious that your own kalesh didn't mention that the female stranded with you was your mate." He cut his smile to Kensie. "Or the females who were so insistent I bring back their friend."

"They don't know all my secrets," Kensie said, turning to face me and jerking my hand down. Then she threw her arms around my neck and pulled me into a hard kiss. Again, I was startled by her forcefulness but quickly allowed myself to be consumed by the sweet taste of her.

I wrapped my arms around her back and lifted her feet from the ground as I parted her lips. Kensie coiled her legs around my waist, hosting herself up and scraping her hands through my hair before gripping my horns tightly.

The pleasure that rocketed through me from the touch of her hands on my horns made me forget that we were being watched by an alien warlord known for being ruthless. I moaned and delved deeper in her mouth, sliding one of my hands up and threading it through her hair. My cock strained painfully in my pants as she writhed in my arms, and I wondered if she'd forgotten we had an audience as well.

I finally tore my lips from hers. She looked at me in a dazed stupor as I let her down, her body sliding down mine.

She managed to straighten her shoulders and face Raas Ronnan. "Do you believe us now?"

His lips twitched. "I believe it makes it easier for me to assign you to shared quarters once we're on my ship." He spun on one heel and started walking away. "Shall we go?"

CHAPTER EIGHTEEN

Kensie

I didn't release Kaos' hand as we stepped into the Vandar ship, although it was a strange sensation to enter something you couldn't see, but the moment I'd passed through the shimmery hull that blended into the background so seamlessly it did appear invisible, I sucked in a breath. The outside of the Vandar warbird, as they called it, was entirely different from the inside, which was dark and massive and echoed with the pounding of storming feet and the deep-throated shouts of more aliens in kilts.

After spending so much time in the bright and luxurious battle arena complex, the Vandar ship seemed brutal and cold. I shivered as we were led across a swaying steel bridge and then up a wide, spiraling staircase. When I tipped my head back, the vast cavity of the ship appeared to extend forever with more suspended walkways and bridges crisscrossing the dark, yawning space.

"I assume you wish to go to your quarters to rest," Ronnan said, flicking a gaze back at us as he strode quickly through his ship.

"How long until we reach my crew mates?" Kaos asked in lieu of an answer.

"The ship with your kalesh is scouting the solar system for the remainder of your ship's escape pods. I have agreed to lend my horde of ships in the battle to defeat the Xulonians, so you will remain with me until our rendezvous time."

I wasn't sure I liked the sound of that, but Kaos nodded. "Then I'd like to continue with you to your command deck and learn more about the plan of attack."

The Vandar nodded, flicking his hand at a warrior behind us. "The Taori will come with me. Escort the female to their quarters."

Kaos dropped my hand as Raas Ronnan continued to stride forward. "I will join you later."

I wasn't sure if we should have kissed again to solidify the story that we were mates, but being the one to initiate three kisses was a bit too much, even though I'd liked kissing Kaos more than I wanted to admit to myself. I trailed the retreating form of the Taori as he fell in step with the Vandar warlord, a flicker of worry teasing the back of my brain.

I didn't know much about the Vandar, but they'd always been spoken about in low, hushed voices, as if saying their name too loudly would make them appear. I'd heard them referred to as vengeful wraiths because they could appear as if they'd materialized from wisps of smoke. Rumor had it they opposed imperial rule and that their wrath was saved for imperial ships and planets under the control of the empire, but there were others who claimed that they doled out punishment indiscriminately.

Following behind the flaxen-haired raider in heavy boots and a kilt that slapped against his muscular thighs, I hoped that we hadn't gone from one captor to another. Kaos seemed confident that Raas Ronnan was in league with his kalesh, but so far I'd seen no proof that the Vandar had come to the aid of the Taori.

"So," I said, hurrying my pace to catch up to my escort, "how did you happen into Xulonian territory? Most ships avoid this system, since the aliens are widely known as xenophobic, and don't allow any other species to enter their space."

He didn't bother to glance at me. "We aren't from this sector. We know nothing of these Xulonians. Since we fly without being seen, we don't worry about being detected."

That made sense, although I was still confused that these were different Vandar. Ronnan had said something about not being the Vandar I was telling Kaos about. But if they weren't the Vandar who were known in this galaxy, who were they?

"But you revealed yourself to the Taori, and they were in Xulonian ships, right? Why would you do that if you didn't want to be detected? You couldn't have known the ships were filled with Taori and humans, could you?"

"You should not underestimate our technology. If our Raas contacted those ships, he had a reason."

"He said you're looking to get revenge on the other Vandar. Did you think they were here?"

The Vandar finally stopped and turned to me. "You ask a lot of questions."

I shrugged and gave him my most charming smile, the one that had usually worked to put new fighters at ease. "We're on the same side, right? I just thought maybe I could help you find the Vandar. I was on the battle moon for a long time and saw a lot of fighters come through."

He cocked a brow at me. "Were any of those fighters Vandar?"

I thought about this, giving him a quick once over. Had I ever seen or heard of a fighter in the arena with platinum hair, a tail, and ink curling across their chest? I shook my head. "No."

He started to walk again, this time faster.

I jogged to catch up. "No Vandar being brought to the battle moon tells you something though. I've seen all kinds of aliens come through. The slavers that procure fighters make sure that there are different species to keep it interesting. If there haven't been any of your species that means the Vandar probably aren't within hunting range of the Hettite slavers."

The Vandar stopped again, pivoting to face me. "Or it means that the Vandar are too ferocious to be captured by these slavers."

I bobbled my head. "Maybe, but they managed to acquire some pretty nasty creatures. What I'm saying is that if you're looking for Vandar here, you're probably looking in the wrong place."

He studied me for a beat then gave a single nod. "That is a rational assumption. I will pass it along to my Raas."

I smiled, pleased that he'd acknowledged that my argument was sound. "I still don't get why your Raas would be so eager to help the Taori. If you're on a revenge mission, won't this be a delay?"

"I do not question my Raas, but it is not unusual for the Vandar to join forces to defeat forces that are subjugating others. It is why we took to the skies after our planet was decimated by the empire."

"So, the Vandar are more like freedom fighters than criminals."

He bristled at this. "We have never been criminals. It is empires who commit the crimes against those they control."

I couldn't disagree with him there. "The Vandar fight for freedom, and the Taori chase a deadly swarm across the galaxy. I guess your species aren't so different."

He grunted at this, his gaze darting behind me. "These are the quarters you will share with your Taori mate."

I spun to face the nondescript gray door that was inset in the wall. The Vandar touched a hand to a panel beside it, the thin seam in the middle parted, and the door glided open. If I'd expected something as spacious and open as the ship itself, I would have been disappointed. There was no soaring ceiling or domed glass like in the arena complex. Instead, the room was compact and dimly lit, with lots of gray and dark metal.

I eyed the single bed, which was larger than a single bunk but didn't seem built for a Taori plus me. I turned to the Vandar. "I'm not sure..." My words faded when I realized that he was gone. Only the tip of his tail was visible as he vanished around a corner.

"I guess it will have to work," I muttered to myself, stepping into the room and letting the door swish shut behind me. I was so tired I barely cared where I slept, as long as I could sleep. I touched a hand to my neck, my fingers feathering over old scars from being shocked as punishment. There were worse things than sparse quarters.

I stumbled to the bed, pulling back the covers and slipping underneath. I could feel the heavy fabric pulling at the sheer remnants of my dress and feel the fabric ripping off, but I didn't care. I didn't even care that Kaos and I were aboard a Vandar ship that was hunting for other Vandar. As I drifted to sleep, I only cared that I was finally free and finally safe.

CHAPTER NINETEEN

Kaos

The iron rattled beneath our feet as I walked with the Vandar through his ship, the hard sound joining the cacophony of thundering footfalls and booming voices that echoed around us. The air was cold, but I welcomed it. From the scant clothing the Vandar wore, I suspected they were a species that also ran hot, as not one of the warriors looked cold as they moved purposefully past me, giving gruff nods of acknowledgment.

I tipped my head back to take in the unusual ship design, gaping at the enormous interior that looked like a dark web of open walkways and twisting stairs. There were few guard rails, and plenty of warriors leaping from one platform to the next.

Watching the Vandar move, their long tails swishing and the flaps of their kilts slapping their thighs, reminded me of my

Taori brothers. We didn't wear kilts, but our tails and horns often made us appear more like beasts. I thought back to the guards at the battle arena referring to Naz and me as beasts. It had rankled me then, but I knew that we relied on our animalistic features to make us the fighters we were. I suspected the same was true of the Vandar, which meant I needed to be wary around them. They would be more dangerous than they appeared.

"Did you crash onto the moon in your pod?" Raas Ronnan cut his gaze to me as he leapt onto a steel platform that moved in a continuous spiral toward the top of the ship. "Like Naz?"

I followed him onto the moving platform as I noted that he knew how my kalesh had ended up on the battle moon, giving more credence to his connection to Naz. That didn't mean I trusted the alien completely.

"Yes, but I was not found as quickly as Kalesh Naz. I wandered on the desert for longer before I was captured."

The Vandar grunted and nodded solemnly. "After encountering Kalesh Naz and your other Taori brothers, we learned of the various moons used by the Xulonians." His top lip curled into a sneer. "It did not take us long to agree to join the fight after hearing the ways these aliens enjoy their torture."

"The other moons are used for things aside from battle?"

"The other Taori with your kalesh had escaped from hunting and lust moons."

My eyebrows popped up in surprise at this. "There is a lust moon?" I wondered which of my brothers had been stranded there.

Ronnan jumped from the spiraling platform and waited for me to join him. "It might sound less harrowing than a battle moon, but the Xulonians pit their captives against each other, prodding them to engage in activities with other captives in order to stay alive—all while they watch and participate as avatars, although they call their version of avatars dimensionals."

The foul tang of bile teased the back of my throat. I was hardly uptight about mating and had enjoyed my fair share of pleasurers when the need arose—like when I was consumed by the Quaibyn—but the idea of unwittingly mating with a red skull in the form of an avatar made my stomach turn and my heart thump faster.

The cool interior of the Vandar ship had helped cool my fever—as had parting ways with Kensie so she could sleep—but I could feel it simmering beneath the surface like a dormant beast. I forced myself to focus on the mission and hope my body would fall in line.

"How many of my fellow Taori have escaped from the moons or been rescued?"

"That I do not know. When your kalesh and I parted ways, he was en route to scour the skies for escape pods that might not have landed on one of the moons."

I pressed my lips together. It had been a while since our ship had been destroyed and the pods deployed. I knew the self-contained vessels had life support, but how long until that ran out?

As if sensing my thoughts, Ronnan placed a hand on my shoulder. "Your kalesh wanted as many searching for those adrift pods as possible, otherwise he would have led the mission to retrieve you himself." The Vandar let a low laugh escape his lips. "He was loath to let me take his place, but he was also convinced you would insist on saving as many Taori as possible."

Naz knew me well. There was no hesitation in my mind that he'd done the right thing. If he'd made the call to leave me on the moon for as long as it took to find all the errant pods, I wouldn't have questioned his decision for a moment.

We approached a wide set of arched doors made of the same dusky-gray metal as most of the ship. They parted for Raas Ronnan, who didn't slow his pace as he strode through them and onto a bustling command deck. I followed, my heart hammering at the familiar sight of warriors at consoles, as beeps and the tapping of fingers filled the air. I could almost convince myself that the warriors with long pale hair and battle axes strapped to their backs were also covered in dark tattoos and had silvery, striped horns curling from their heads.

Heads swiveled at out arrival and every Vandar on the bridge rapped their heels together sharply at the arrival of their leader. He took a position on an elevated, curved platform that overlooked the half-moon shaped command deck, and he motioned for me to join him. A wall of glass stretched in front of us, giving a view of the desert landscape I wouldn't be sad to leave.

The inky blue sky had faded as the sun teased the horizon, sending warm gold washing across the sand dunes. If I didn't know how brutal the surface would be soon after the sun rose, I would have found the scene beautiful.

"Take us out of here," he commanded, stealing a quick glance at a nearby Vandar at a standing console. "*Vaes!*"

A murmur of excitement went through the Vandar as the ship rumbled and then jerked as it lifted from the surface. Sand kicked up in a blinding swirl below, but it didn't reach the height of the viewing glass as we briskly rose. In the distance, I could see the sparkling domes of the battle arena glittering as the sun danced off the colorful glass. How could something so cruel appear like a jewel on the sand?

Memories of being dragged into the dank dungeon sent fresh

waves of fury through me and heat flushed my skin. So long on the desert had made me almost mad with heat and thirst, and it had prompted my fever to rage in my body. I'd been barely more than a rutting beast when I'd encountered Naz, and now thoughts of that made my heart race and black dots dance before my eyes.

"I promised your kalesh that I would do one more thing after I ensured you and the female were safe." Ronnan gave a slight nod to the closest warrior as the ship hovered over the moon's surface.

Now that the darkness wasn't a shroud to hide behind, it was easy to see the caravan snaking across the desert toward the mountains. I'd suspected that the group was guards searching for us, but now I could see it was a motley group of various aliens. The fighters we'd released from the cells! They'd escaped from the arena and were heading for shelter.

Before I could explain who they were to Raas Ronnan, a smaller ship became visible and landed beside them.

"Your kalesh didn't think the other fighters should be abandoned," the Vandar warlord said. "We're rescuing them and letting them join in our fight."

I watched with some satisfaction as the tiny figures rushed toward the Vandar transport. I wanted to ask what would happen to the guards and Xulonian we'd left behind at the arena, but the Vandar warbird was already pivoting to fully face the sprawling complex. My fingers twitched with the urge to reach for a weapon, my instinct to lash out at the aliens who'd imprisoned me and my kalesh so powerful I was practically panting.

"Do it," Ronnan growled.

Weapons fire erupted from the Vandar ship, red streaks arching through the air and landing on the battle arena. The domes exploded as fireballs billowed into the air followed by plumes of black smoke. Even the warbird shuddered from the explosions, and I held my arms out to steady myself.

When there was nothing left of the arena, Ronnan folded his arms over his chest and released a satisfied grunt. “Now we rejoin the others and continue our war against the Xulonians.” He turned on his heel and eyed me. “After you tell me why you lied about the female being your mate.”

CHAPTER TWENTY

Kensie

His hands were strong and warm as they moved up my body, his familiar touch rousing me from my deep sleep. I laughed sleepily and rolled over, flapping one hand to wave him off. “I’m sleeping, you brute.”

“Brute?” His chuckle was warm and rich as it slid into my bones and made my pulse flutter.

“Yes,” I mumbled. “You’re a big brute who would rather torment me than rest up for your fight tomorrow.”

Even through the darkness, I could make out the shape of him as he held himself over me—broad shoulders and short hair that curled around the nape of his neck. “Sleep so I can fight some repulsive alien tomorrow, or spend the night tangled up with the most beautiful attendant in the entire arena.”

I giggled, the compliment making my cheeks flush. "Now you're a brute and a liar."

"I would never lie." He bent down and nipped at the soft flesh of my throat. "You're the most beautiful woman I've ever known, and I count myself the luckiest man alive that I got sent to this arena so I could meet you."

"A brute, a liar, and insane." A moan slipped from my lips as his warm breath tickled my neck. "No one considers themselves lucky for getting brought to the battle moon."

"I do." He continued nipping his way down my throat, the soft bites turning into kisses that he scattered across my collarbone. "I'd rather have this short, perfect time with you than a lifetime of boring."

"You keep saying that." Even as heat gathered in my belly, fear tingled across my bare skin.

"I mean it. I know what we have won't last forever, but shouldn't we take every amazing moment of it?"

He was right. We never knew which fight might be his last, even though he was skilled and tough, but we did have these moments. I sighed, running my hands through his hair. "We should."

His growl in response sent shivers of pleasure through me. My fingers brushed against something cool and ridged, and I curled my fingers around curved horns. Wait, what?

He lifted his head, his iridescent-blue eyes glimmering at me as he shifted his body over me, his knee parting my legs and his tail trailing up the inside of one of my legs.

"Kaos?"

His only answer was another velvety growl as he lowered his mouth to my shoulder, his tongue so hot it felt like it was searing my skin.

I bolted up in bed, gasping and kicking at the heavy blanket. "What the hell?"

It took me a beat to recall that I wasn't in the arena complex or even on the alien moon at all. I was in a Vandar warbird after they'd rescued us from the surface. A chill went through me at the thought of being guests of the Vandar, not something I ever could have imagined before.

It took me another moment to realize that the Vandar ship was shaking, and from the ambient light recessed in the ceiling I could make out the utilitarian furniture vibrating. I pushed aside the dream I'd had, as it became clear that it had been a dream. No one was in the compact quarters. Not the fighter I'd once loved, and not Kaos.

I released a breath, not sure if I was relieved or disappointed that Kaos wasn't in bed with me. The dream had been so vivid, and my fingers still buzzed as if I'd been rubbing them along the ridged stripes of his horn.

I shook my head, as if I could shake the memories free from my brain. It had been a long time since I'd dreamt about Mick, and even longer since I'd remembered the things he used to say to me. I'd forced myself to forget them, because for a long time, I'd been angry at him for dying and for making me believe him. I'd bought into his belief that our brief time together was enough for a lifetime, because he'd believed it so strongly. It was impossible not to be swept up in his enthusiasm for the idyllic time we'd shared, because he'd made every moment magical. He'd made me believe that perfect love couldn't be limited by time—until he'd died and left me to pick up the pieces of my broken heart.

Dreaming about him and remembering how happy we'd been for that brief time hadn't made me sad this time, as it had when I'd first dreamt about Mick. For some reason, thoughts of him didn't make my heart ache so painfully anymore. They actually made me smile.

I touched a hand to my cheek, surprised that it was wet.

But these were happy tears. I finally felt the same gratitude he'd always talked about. There was no longer a hollow ache in my heart. There was only joy that I'd experienced so much happiness in such a dark place.

"I guess I'm as crazy as you, Mick," I whispered, "because I finally feel lucky."

The ship shuddered again, and I kicked off the covers entirely and swung my feet to the floor. When I stood, my dress fell from my body and settled into a sad pile of dirty, torn fabric.

"That dress wasn't so lucky," I muttered, scanning the room for anything else to wear.

I spotted a towel hanging in the attached bathroom and snatched it from the hook, wrapping it around my body and tucking it under my arm. It wasn't the height of fashion, but it would do while I figured out if the Vandar ship was under attack.

I made my way to the door and fumbled around the side of it until it glided open. The shaking had stopped, but I still poked my head outside. There was no one in sight, which was good because that meant they hadn't posted a guard outside my room. I let out another sigh as it sank in that I wasn't anyone's captive anymore.

The only problem with no guard was that there was no one to ask why the ship had been shaking so violently. Were we under attack, or did Vandar ships just rumble a lot? I spotted a tall Vandar storming down a curling staircase at the end of the open-air corridor and stepped out of my quarters to wave him down.

"Excuse me," I called out, but my voice cracked, and he didn't hear me.

I stepped further into the corridor, darting my head in all directions, but there was no one else. I groaned and turned back to the door, but it had closed. I waved my hand around the arch, patted my palm to each side, and even attempted to pry the seam in the middle apart, but it wouldn't budge.

I closed my eyes as I leaned my forehead against the cool steel of the door. I was stuck outside my quarters on a Vandar ship in nothing but a towel.

CHAPTER TWENTY-ONE

Kaos

"Lied?" My voice emerged as a rasp as I faced the Vandar warlord.

Raas Ronnan held my gaze for a long time before he eyed me up and down. "Your kalesh told me that when he last saw you the mating fever had turned you into a desperate creature who was afraid of his own actions. You asked Naz to kill you so you wouldn't dishonor yourself."

My face burned at those memories.

"When I saw you with the human, you did not seem in the midst of an all-consuming fever, so I assumed what you told me was true." He inclined his head at me. "But now, I fear you might not have told me everything."

I felt the eyes of his fellow warriors on me even though the ship was in the process of bursting through the moon's atmosphere and into space. A Taori who might or might not be in the middle of an ancient mating fever was probably not something that happened on their command deck every day.

"*Vaes!*" Raas Ronnan spun around and waved for me to follow him as he took long steps toward a door inset in the side of the command deck.

I was glad to follow and be free of the curious looks from the broad-shouldered warriors with white-blond hair. The narrow door opened for Ronnan, and he entered the room with me close on his heels.

"My strategy room might be better for a conversation of this nature," he said, taking a seat behind a glossy desk and motioning for me to take the high-backed chair across from it.

I sat on the edge without my back touching. My heart was thundering in my chest as I quickly scanned the walls for any weapons or indications that the strategy room was, in fact, a torture chamber. I was a guest on the Vandar ship, and I was taking the warlord at his word that he'd rescued me at the bidding of Kalesh Naz. I held no position of authority, and I was in no position to make demands—or be caught lying.

"I do not blame you," Ronnan said. "From what I could tell, you were only agreeing with the female. The question is, why did she feel compelled to say you were her mate? Had you rebuffed her advances? Had you already cured your mating fever with another female?"

I shook my head vigorously. "I do not know why she made the claim, unless she knows something about the Vandar I do not."

I held my breath, shocked that I'd actually implied the Vandar might have a bad reputation with females and how the warlord might react.

Instead of being angry or insulted, he grinned. "I suspect she knows much more about the Vandar's reputation. The original Vandar are not known for taking prisoners, although they are known for frequenting pleasure planets. Maybe she was afraid we'd mistake her for a pleasurer."

"She was a captive in the battle arena just like Naz and I were, but the females there did not attend the males in that way."

He nodded. "I was told as much by Naz and his mate." His brows lifted. "There is no doubt that those two are mated."

I thought back to seeing Tyrria with my kalesh. He'd already been as devoted to the pink-haired female as he was to his Taori brothers, which was saying something.

"If you are not mated with the human, then you are still experiencing this Quaibyn?" His gaze cut to my chest as sweat rolled down it in rivulets. "It was hard not to notice your reaction to the destruction of the arena."

I swiped a palm across my slick chest. "I am, although I have been able to slow its effects by removing myself from the female's presence. The cooler temperature on your ship also helps."

He nodded. "But if you do not break this fever by mating, you can become violent or go mad?"

Kalesh Naz had told him a lot about the Quaibyn. I bit my bottom lip, not liking where this conversation was going but also understanding his position as the leader of his warriors. "I am rarely a threat to anyone but females, and I haven't seen any of those on your sky ship."

Ronnan shook his head. "The Vandar have never allowed females on our warbirds, unless the Raas chooses to have his Raisa join him, but that is exceedingly rare. Even fierce Vandar females don't enjoy life on a ship of all warriors."

"It is the same with the Taori. There are female warriors on our home world, but none who traveled with us on our endless mission that will have no return."

"Your madness does not provoke violence?" He met my

gaze with a solemn one of his own. "I cannot risk a skilled warrior running loose on my ship without control of reason or temper. My Vandar raiders are not ones to shrink from a fight when provoked, and the last thing I want is a ship in turmoil."

I considered his words carefully then thought about Kensie. Raas Ronnan had assigned us to share a single, compact room when he believed we were a mated couple. I could not safely stay with her without fear of losing control.

"The only one in danger from me is the female." I dropped my gaze, the shame of the words washing over me. "I would rather die than betray my Taori honor, so I request that I be separated from her."

The warlord nodded. "That can be done. I arranged for food and drink to be taken to her, so she will be comfortable until we can arrange for her to be moved to one of the ships with her fellow females from the arena."

An ache stabbed my heart at the prospect of not seeing her again. It was for the best, I told myself. Even now, my body felt like it was being shot through with an electrical current and my limbs hummed with an almost uncontrollable desire. Even thinking of her made my cock twitch to life and an unwanted growl rumble in my chest.

"Good. Please do not place my quarters near hers. It would be best if there was no way for me to run into her." I didn't add that if she was close to me, I might be able to detect her scent.

Raas Ronnan stood. "For her safety, the safety of my crew, and your own well-being, I feel compelled to place you under guard until we can find you some relief or return you to your Taori."

I accepted this with a grunt as I stood. "I have no issue with that. We will be rejoining the others soon, won't we?"

"Soon enough," the Vandar said as we were interrupted by a beep at his door. He frowned. "*Vaes!*"

The door slid open, and a warrior entered, clicking his heels and squaring his shoulders.

"You have a good reason for coming to my strategy room?" Ronnan asked, coming around to the front of his desk.

"I was tasked with delivering the food and drink to our female guest." The Vandar was clearly young. His voice trembled and his gaze was locked over Raas Ronnan's head.

"Is there a problem?" the Raas asked.

"Is she well?" I asked, wondering if she might be experiencing after-effects from our ordeal on the alien moon.

"She is..." the Vandar swallowed noticeably, "not there."

Ronnan stiffened. "Not there? Where could she be?"

My protective instincts flared to life. Kensie was wandering in a Vandar warbird alone.

The Vandar warrior held out a handful of fabric. "All I found of hers inside the room was this."

I instantly recognized the remains of her dress.

My pulse quickened. She was wandering alone—and unclothed.

CHAPTER TWENTY-TWO

Kensie

This was a disaster. I continued to fumble around the door but couldn't get it to open. I didn't know if it was biometrically linked to Vandar DNA, or if there was some kind of tapping combination I hadn't noticed when I'd been shown to my quarters, but the door was not budging.

I groaned and turned around. At this point, I didn't know if I wanted a Vandar warrior to happen by. I was wearing nothing but a towel, and I had no room to dart back into. I'd noticed enough of the Vandars' curious stares and roaming gazes as I'd been led through the ship to think that wandering half-naked wasn't a great idea. Not that I thought the aliens would rip off my towel and pin me to a wall, but I did not welcome their hungry looks—or the embarrassment of admitting I'd been boneheaded enough to lock myself out of my room with no clothes. If I'd hoped to impress the Vandar with my human intelligence, this was not the way to do it.

I swiveled my head in both directions. Standing outside the door wasn't getting me anywhere, and I didn't know how to find Kaos or the Vandar warlord. Not that I especially wanted to run into him. He'd looked at me like I was good enough to eat when he'd found me on the moon's surface.

I shook my head, abandoning all thoughts of searching for the bridge. What I needed to find was clothing. Maybe there was a laundry department on board or a place that stocked uniforms. I took off down one side of the corridor, retracing my steps from the lower section of the vessel. My limited experience in spaceships had taught me that most of the utilitarian rooms were located below, so that was where I was headed.

I ran on my toes, glad I was barefoot and moving almost silently, although the steel floor was cold. The entire ship was colder than I was accustomed to, and I wished that the towel reached lower on my thighs.

"I must have grabbed the Vandar version of a hand towel," I muttered to myself with a shiver.

A pair of Vandar approached from the end of the long, open corridor, but they were deep in conversation with their heads bowed as their legs ate up the distance between us. I suppressed the impulse to make a startled sound, as I ducked down a side hallway and flattened myself to the wall. I held my breath as they thundered past, only daring to exhale once the sound of their heavy footfall had faded.

How was I going to make my way through a ship that was almost entirely open without being seen? I dragged a hand through my hair, noticing that the curls had dried in a mass of frizz. Another reason not to want to be seen—my current disheveled state might be terrifying. I didn't consider myself vain, but no girl wants a guy to recoil in horror when they see her.

One advantage to the open layout was that it was easy to see and hear anyone approaching. That, and the Vandar raiders seemed preoccupied as they stormed through the ship, and so far they didn't seem to be searching for me.

"Clothes," I said to myself as I poked my head from the narrow offshoot corridor. "I need to find clothes."

I hurried down the length of the passageway and glanced around furtively before holding my towel tight and rushing down a coiling staircase. Once down it, I dashed across a suspended bridge and down another hallway before having to hide in a recessed alcove as more Vandar warriors passed.

I was doing a decent job of remembering the route I'd taken to reach my quarters and backtracking it. At least, I thought I was. The Vandar warbird was such a complicated labyrinth that wound through a vast center chasm that it was hard to tell one suspended bridge or spiraling, iron stairway from another. At least I could peer up to tell that I was getting farther from the top of the ship.

By this time, my feet were icy, and my skin was covered in chill bumps. I didn't know how the Vandar didn't freeze, considering they wore only skirts made of leather. As soon as I wondered this, my stomach sank. They only wore leather kilts. They wouldn't have any use for a laundry, and the only uniforms they'd be storing were more skirts sized for Vandar. The only way I could make one of those work was if I wore it around my chest. Even then, it might barely cover the crucial bits. Not to mention, the kilts were made from hanging strips of leather. Not exactly the coverage I needed.

"I'd be better off sticking with the towel," I grumbled as I realized my plan was a disaster.

I slumped against the wall, wondering what to do next.

Should I make myself known to the next Vandar I saw? I cringed at this. I was still barely dressed, and now I was in the bowels of the ship.

I took a deep breath to gather my courage, and my nose twitched. Did I smell food? My stomach grumbled in response. I hadn't eaten in ages, and the soggy moss did not count, no matter how many nutrients Kaos insisted it had. I inhaled again. That was definitely the aroma of bread.

As if drawn to the food, I found myself moving toward the yeasty scent. I made my way down another level to where the corridor was tight, and the sounds of clanging and shouting echoed down it. Unless I was very mistaken, I was near the kitchens.

I practically ran toward food, only stopping when I was outside the wide, open doorway. There was a rolling cart stacked high with trays and baskets, long loaves of bread protruding from rough woven cloth draped over a basket. I slid out one of the loaves, almost moaning with pleasure from the warmth of it.

Grateful I didn't have to enter the kitchen and ask for food in my current state, I slipped into a nearby storage room with my bread, noticing that this door opened automatically for me. A quick glance told me that this was where the Vandar stored casks of wine or ale. The massive wooden casks were stacked on their rounded bellies in a storage unit built into the walls, although a few were sitting upright. They were as high as my waist and provided good cover, so I could hide from sight while eating my bread.

I slid down one and sat with my back to it and hidden from the door as I tore off a hunk of bread with my teeth. The crusty crust splintered in my mouth, sending crumbs spilling onto my lap, but I didn't care. The inside of the bread was soft and steamy, my tongue burning from the heat. I was too hungry to care about that, either.

I'd devoured almost half the loaf before I realized that I wasn't alone in the room. I'd been so preoccupied with chewing and distracted by the muffled sounds from the nearby kitchen that I hadn't picked up on the burst of savory steam that now suffused the air and deep breathing that wasn't my own. The door had opened at some point, but had someone come inside? I froze, swallowing my mouthful of bread as silently as possible as I listened for movement. Had someone heard me, or were they just coming for a cask of something?

I'd started to relax my shoulders, convinced that I'd imagined the breathing when a thick hand grasped my arm and hauled me to my feet. Both the bread and my towel dropped to the floor.

CHAPTER TWENTY-THREE

Kaos

I snatched the fabric of Kenzie's dress from the Vandar warrior. "Where was this?"

The pale-haired male blinked at me, his eyes wide. "On the floor by the bed."

Her dress had already been in tatters when we arrived. I didn't doubt that it had fallen from her in shreds, but if that was the case, why had she left the room?

My mind raced with possibilities even as primal protective urges flooded my body. Was she trying to leave the ship? She must know that we were in-flight. There was no way off unless it was by transport, and as far as I knew, she couldn't fly.

"The female cannot leave the ship," Raas Ronnan said, once again anticipating my thoughts. "No ships depart without my authorization, and there is no other exit." He paused and tilted his head. "Except by airlock."

"She has no reason to want to leave," I said. "She wanted off the moon as much as I did."

But was that true? Hadn't Kensie complained that I'd dragged her into the desert when life in the arena complex was luxurious? Well, there was no arena for her to return to now, and all of her friends were with Kalesh Naz and my Taori brothers.

"We will find her," Ronnan assured me, turning his attention to the warrior who'd delivered the news. "Send a search party to comb the ship."

He snapped his heels together in salute. "It is done, Raas."

"When you find her, bring her to me," Ronnan added as the warrior turned to the door.

This made the hairs on the back of my neck stand on end. Why did he want her brought to him? Now my possessive desires awakened. Since Raas Ronnan knew she wasn't actually my mate, did he consider her fair game? I knew little about the Vandar, but Kensie had called them raiders. Would the warlord now consider her part of the bounty from the moon? Was anything salvaged automatically his to possess?

My mind instantly propelled me backward in time, and I was standing in the banqueting hall on Taor. Candles burned in sconces on the wall, flickering as they illuminated the long, carved tables where warriors dined after a grueling training session. The high-ceilinged, beamed hall echoed with the rumble of voices and was filled with the heady scent of grilled meat and pungent wine. But all those sensations had faded away as soon as I'd seen it—my intended mate stealing a heated glance at my brother.

If it had only been a glance, I might have brushed it off as me being paranoid. But then she'd brushed her hand across his as she'd passed by him, her slender fingers lingering within his palm for a moment. It had been the familiar touch of a lover, and I'd instantly known that both my love and my brother had betrayed me.

My skin prickled as I recalled the feeling of having a female I'd love snatched from me. I wouldn't let it happen again. Not that Kensie was mine. Her kiss had only been to convince the Vandar we were mated, a fact I had to remind myself of every time I thought of her soft, eager lips on mine. We were not truly mates, and I'd sworn I'd never allow a female to get close enough to risk my heart again. I curled my hands into fists as I thought of the maddening human and how she rattled the foundations of my self-control. Even though I would not allow myself to think of her as anything but an obligation, I would not have the Vandar take her from me.

"I will join the search party," I said, following the warrior to the door of Raas Ronnan's strategy room.

"Didn't we agree that you would be safer under armed guard?"

I didn't remember agreeing to an *armed* guard, although it would be naïve to think any Vandar wouldn't be carrying one of their sizable axes. Suddenly, I wondered how many of his precautions were for security, and how many were to keep me neutralized.

"That was before the human I swore to protect went missing." I twisted my head to meet his gaze. "I need to make sure she is safe."

Raas Ronnan seemed to study me for a while. "I do not know whether to believe that you aren't mates, or to think you couldn't be anything but."

"I assure you that she is not my mate. That does not mean I don't wish to make sure she is safe. I vowed to get her to safety. That vow does not break because we are on your ship and benefitting from your hospitality."

He grunted, waving a hand at me. "Your kalesh told me you

had a will of iron and would never give up. Go find the human. Then we will confine you until you can be reunited with your Taori crew."

I didn't respond. Instead, I gave him a curt nod and followed the Vandar from the room. He quickly assembled a search party from the command deck, and we descended into the shadowy depths of the warbird.

"We'll start at the quarters she left," the Vandar leading the group announced.

It wasn't a bad plan. I hadn't seen the quarters assigned to us—even though now they would only be Kenzie's quarters, and I'd be far from her with guards manning my door—and I followed the group down winding stairs and groaning bridges. We reached an unassuming arched door set into the gray walls. The Vandar touched the wall and the door slid open to reveal a small, spartan compartment. The covers on the bed were pushed back but otherwise, there was no sign that she'd been there.

Except for the smell. I breathed in, detecting the distinctive scent of her. If the Vandar could smell her, they didn't mention it, but I suspected my abilities were only because of the Quaibyn.

"We should split up," I said, causing the Vandar to turn toward me. "There are so many places she could go. If we stay together, it might take too long."

The Vandar in charge made a noise that told me he agreed, but he didn't like it. "Fine. Split up." He eyed me. "Do you need a partner? You don't know the warbird."

I shook my head. "I'll be fine. I've been on lots of ships. I always manage to find my way around."

He nodded, and I knew he was glad he wasn't going to have to be my escort. No doubt he thought I'd slow him down.

I let the others rush off in search of Kensie while I merely inhaled deeply again. Breathing in the smell of her made my heart thrum in my chest and my blood run hot through my veins. I shouldn't be searching for her. Not in my state. But my state was the reason I would be able to find her before the rest. I might not be mated to her, but her scent was impressed upon me.

I followed the sweet trace of her down the hallways and deep into the cavernous ship. She'd certainly gone down, but why? I couldn't believe she was attempting an escape, but it was undeniable that I was following her trail to the depths of the ship which held the hangar bay.

When I reached a few levels above the base of the vessel, I stopped. Here her scent mixed with the heady aroma of food. I nearly stumbled toward the savory smells emanating from the clattering sounds of the kitchens. When I reached the open mouth of the room where cooks were shouting orders as steam billowed from the door, I stopped.

Kensie had been here. I heaved in ragged breaths, as the combination of her smell and that of the Vandar cuisine made me lightheaded. I snatched a loaf of bread from a nearby cart and bit into it. I was so ravenous, it only took me moments to devour the bread, leaving a smattering of crumbs at my feet.

Once my hunger was sated, I tipped my head back and inhaled again. Then I allowed myself to be led to a nearby room and opened the door. I paused on the threshold, noticing the powerful aroma of Kensie even more than the soft sounds of movement from within. Casks of strong wine lined the walls —I could smell the pungent, fruitiness through the wooden barrels—and several were upright, blocking my view of her. But even without seeing her, I could hear the crunch of the bread.

She wasn't running away. She'd gone looking for food. Since I'd just made quick work of a loaf of bread myself, I couldn't blame her for being hungry. Any anger or frustration I'd felt when I suspected she might be trying to escape immediately evaporated like the savory steam from the kitchens.

I tried to temper my other emotions—desire, hunger, protectiveness—but sweat rolled down my bare skin and my fingers vibrated with the need to touch her. I should have backed away and alerted the others to her location. I shouldn't be the one to take her back.

I knew better than to trust myself in my current state of fever, and I knew better than to trust a female. I'd been badly burned by a female who'd sworn she loved me. This human had made no such promises, yet I couldn't stop myself from thinking that she would never willfully hurt me. But what if I was wrong?

Then I thought about Raas Ronnan's request that she be brought to him. I might have sworn off forming an attachment to another female, but that didn't mean I would stand by and let Kensie be claimed by another. The idea of the Vandar's hands on her made me want to put my fist through a wall. That was *not* happening.

A growl built in my throat as a possessive urge washed over me like a haze. I reached around the wooden cask hiding her and lifted her into the air. Her eyes gaped as the loaf of bread she'd been clutching fell to the floor, followed by the towel that had been wrapped around her body.

CHAPTER TWENTY-FOUR

Kensie

I gaped up, expecting to see a Vandar raider, or maybe even an irate cook who'd realized I'd stolen his bread. When I saw it was Kaos, I relaxed—until I realized my towel was now in a heap on the floor.

His hot gaze traveled down my body, greedily devouring the sight of me like he was the starving one and I was the crusty baguette. He let go of my arm and snatched back his hand as if it was burned, backing away from me.

I hurriedly gathered my towel from the floor and fumbled to wrap it around myself again. I considered picking up the bread, but I wasn't *that* hungry anymore. "What are you doing here? How did you find me?"

"What am *I* doing here?" His chest hitched as he braced his trembling hands on his hips. "You left your quarters."

The door muffled the noise and smell of the kitchens, but

Kaos's entrance had brought a cloud of fragrant steam. I breathed it in, my mind wandering to the food they were preparing and wondering how I could get more, but I returned my focus to the Taori, who was clearly upset with me.

I shook my head. "I got locked out of my quarters. Big difference. I don't know the deal with the doors around here, but they don't automatically open every time."

"You could have asked to be let back in."

I waved a hand at my towel. "In this? I don't know if you've noticed, but the only people on this ship are enormous guys who look like they haven't seen a female in ages."

He grunted, his gaze darting around the room as he started to pace. "No one knew what happened to you. We found your torn dress and thought..."

I cocked my head at him. "That dress literally fell off me. I'm shocked it lasted as long as it did. That's why I grabbed a towel. I stuck my head out of the room when the ship started shaking and then got stuck outside and couldn't get back in. What did you think happened?"

His jaw was clenched as he snapped his gaze to me. "I thought you might be trying to leave."

"Leave?" Was he kidding? He seemed a bit manic, and even in the dim lighting, he appeared to be covered in sweat. "We're on a spaceship. Where would I go?"

He jerked his head away. "You were angry I saved you and took you onto the desert."

"That was before. I'm grateful you saved me." I crossed to him, pressing a hand to his slick chest, startled by how hot his skin was to the touch. "I'm not going anywhere, and I wouldn't leave without you."

He closed a hand around mine. "You should not touch me."

"This again?"

He pried my hand from him and stumbled back. "I

shouldn't have come searching for you. I knew the temptation would be too much." He scraped a hand roughly through his hair. "I need to return you to your quarters, and I will go to mine. "

I squinted at him. "I thought we were sharing quarters, since the Vandar think we're mates."

He bent over at the waist, bracing his hands on his knees. "They no longer believe that. Raas Ronnan saw through our deception because he noticed the symptoms of the Quaibyn."

I looked at Kaos—really looked at him. The parts of his skin not covered in tattoos looked like they were blistered. His hands shook, the pulse on the sides of his neck throbbed, and he was emitting a low guttural sound that was half growl and half moan of despair.

"You're worse," I said. "A lot worse."

He curled his hands into fists as he straightened. His body quivered from the effort to control his carnal urges. "I can't control it. I thought I could master myself enough to return you to your quarters, but you should go." He glanced up at me, his hair falling over his eyes, which were wild. The blue that was usually so bright had been swallowed up by the molten black pupils, and his eyes were dark pools of fire. "Go now, before it's too late."

My pulse jackknifed as I watched him, but it wasn't fear that welled up in me. It was compassion and my own desire. I approached him, resting my hands lightly on his chest. "It's already too late for me."

He twisted his head to one side, as if using the last remnants of self-control. "What?"

The blood pounded in my ears as I met his tormented gaze. Did I know what I was doing? I'd promised myself I would never allow myself to get attached to another warrior again, but if I did what I was thinking of doing, a connection with

Kaos would be inevitable. As much as I thought I could erect a wall to protect my heart, I knew it would be a lie. If I did this, there would be no going back.

My hands trembled as they rested on his hot skin, and I focused on the enormous skull marked in dark ink from his chest to his abdomen. The mouth was elongated as if in a silent scream, and I wondered if this was how Kaos felt. How much pain was he hiding?

"It doesn't have to be a lie," I said, the words spilling from my mouth in a rush. "What we told Raas Ronnan about being mates. That doesn't have to be a lie."

The growl that had been vibrating his chest curled from his gritted teeth. "You do not know what you're saying. You don't know what you're offering."

My heart was knocking against my ribs, doubt niggling at me, but his words fired me with determination. Who was he to say what I understood? It had taken enough courage to say the words in the first place, but being second-guessed made me want to knee him in the balls.

"I'm not some innocent female who doesn't know how the universe works, Kaos. I know exactly what it means if I help you cure your mating fever." I calmed my tone, moving my hands gently over his skin. "I want this. I want you."

He squeezed his eyes shut. "You do not have to do this. I can find another way." He shook his head brusquely. "This is not why I saved you."

"If this is about your Taori honor, you don't have to worry about that. I know you've been fighting this. If you weren't honorable, you'd have fucked me in those tunnels that turned out to be the insides of a sand creature."

Another pained sound escaped from him.

"I'm not only doing this for you." My throat tightened. "I'm also doing this for me. It's been a really long time since I've felt anything for anyone. I let grief deaden me for so long that I forgot what it was like to feel alive. I thought that if I didn't feel anything, I couldn't get hurt." I drew in a steadying breath. "But that's no way to live. Someone told me once that it's better to experience a little bit of joy than a whole lot of nothing special, even if it hurts like hell when you lose it."

Kaos opened his eyes and met my gaze. "I would never hurt you—and you will not lose me."

I inhaled sharply, surprised by his words, and gasping as he lifted me by the waist and hoisted me onto one of the standing casks. I gripped his horns for balance, and a dark purr buzzed my fingertips.

"You *are* going to feel this, female," he growled as he spread my legs.

"I'm counting on it." Then I yanked his head to me and crushed my mouth to his.

CHAPTER TWENTY-FIVE

Kaos

Her kiss sent a jolt through me, startling me, even though it wasn't the first time. Kensie kissing me was starting to become a habit I could live with. I sank into the feel of her soft lips yielding to me as I delved into her mouth with my tongue. If her mouth tasted so intoxicating, what kind of tantalizing honey was between her legs?

As I stroked my tongue against hers, I couldn't stop myself from imagining that I was stroking her sex. My skin prickled with the need to do more than kiss her, even though her mouth was heaven. I moved my hands down her body, caressing her through the towel until I reached her open legs.

I could not resist her any longer. Not when she gave herself to me so freely. This was what she wanted. I saw it in the frantic heat of her eyes as the words fell in a desperate jumble from her mouth. I listened to her words—understanding her admission of being deadened by grief and wanting to feel again—but the roar of pounding blood in my ears made it hard to understand every word.

What I heard was that she wanted this, even if it wouldn't last, even if it was only a bit of happiness, a stolen moment of fun. She would rather risk the pain when it was over than never experience the joy.

This I understood. I'd been careful not to let my heart become entangled with a female since I'd been betrayed, but this would not be any kind of commitment I needed to fear. Kensie did not want my heart. She wanted some pleasure to make her feel alive again.

When I'd said she would not lose me, her eyes had widened. Maybe it had been too much, but it was difficult to temper my instinct to protect her, even from my own need to retreat. Rational thoughts drifted from my mind as I broke our kiss and knelt between her legs. She wanted to feel alive, and I would make her feel so much she'd beg me to have mercy on her.

A violent growl wracked my body and sent a shudder through me. As much as I needed to fuck the fever from me, I couldn't resist tasting her. My heightened sense of smell and taste drove me to force her legs apart. The towel parted, as did her creamy thighs, and I let out a desperate sound as I breathed in the sweet musk of her sex. Her skin was smooth and bare, like pink petals of a flower opening to me as she moaned and leaned back.

With a gruff growl, I buried my head between her legs and dragged my tongue through her slickness. I could taste everything—the water from the spring-fed pool, the natural warm scent of her skin, her desire—and it sent ravenous hunger arrowing through me. My cock thickened, aching to be freed and sheathed within her heat, and my body trembled from the strain of resisting the instinct to plunge myself deep, but that had to wait. I was overcome by a primal need to have my fill of her taste and feel her ecstasy on my tongue.

I closed my eyes as I stroked my tongue between her legs, letting her breathy sounds and urgent movements guide me. Slipping my hands under her ass, I forced her thighs to drop open even further for me as I slid my tongue deep inside her. Then I lapped at the juices coating her and dampening her soft skin, eager to have her scent on my face and imprinted in my brain.

She was mine now. I'd breathed in the aroma of her skin enough times to burn it into my mind but now I was drinking her in and letting her scent mark me. A possessive thrill sent spots dancing behind my eyelids, and I was dizzy with the heady perfume of her.

I dragged the flat of my tongue up the length of her sex, pausing at the firm bundle of nerves. Her ass twitched beneath me, but I tightened my grip on it. She would not escape me until I'd felt her body convulse with pleasure.

I slid one thick finger inside her as I swirled my tongue around her nub, reveling in her throaty moan that filled the room. I moved my finger rhythmically as I worked her with my tongue, her gasps and groans growing louder. I didn't care if anyone heard us. A part of me wanted them to, wanted the Vandar to know that she was mine and I was laying claim to her body.

"I didn't know an alien warrior would do this," Kensie said between stolen breaths.

I lifted my mouth from her for a beat. "You thought I'd want to rut you like a wild beast?" Not that that sounded like a bad idea, but I shook my head. "And miss how sweet you taste?

No, I have to get you ready to take me. When I'm done, you will beg me to fuck you."

She groaned at this. I ran my other hand up her body, pulling the towel aside as I cupped one full breast and then the other. I opened my eyes, staring across the curves of her, and sliding my hand up to her neck and finally her plump mouth.

Kensie lifted her head, her eyes half-lidded with desire, and gave me a wicked grin as she parted her lips and took one of my fingers into her mouth. She sucked on it, dragging it fully inside. I jerked from the shock of her hot mouth and the sensation of her lips on me as mine were on her. My cock was rock hard as I watched her slide my finger in and out of her puckered, pink lips.

I lifted my own head from her. "Is that how you want to take my cock? Do you want to take it all, greedy female?"

She nodded, sucking harder on my finger. My eyes nearly rolled into the back of my head. The human was driving me wild.

I pulled my finger from her mouth, trailing it down the length of her lush body, and slid it inside her. She sucked in a sharp breath when I added the second finger, but she shifted her hips and her eyes flashed in challenge. "More."

My heart thundered as my body raged with heat. Even the cool air of the storage room and the sharp tang of the aging wine didn't staunch my fever. I needed to hold on until I got what I wanted, even though I was lightheaded from the sounds and tastes of her. I returned my mouth to her, lavishing her with my tongue as I moved my fingers inside her, stretching her and preparing her to take my cock.

Kensie grasped my horns as her body began to tremble, her small fingers stroking the sensitive stripes. It was almost too much to withstand, but I was so close. She was so close.

She looped her legs around my shoulders and tightened her grip on my horns. I slid my fingers from her and bucked up, standing and taking her with me as she sat on my shoulders with her legs spread around my face. She screamed, but I didn't know if it was from the shock of being in the air or because I was sucking hard on her slick nub and her legs were shaking.

The ceiling in the storage room was high enough that her head didn't brush the top, but I moved a few steps so that her back was to the rows of wooden casks in case she decided to let go. I grabbed her ass from behind and held her to me as she rode my face using my horns for balance, rocking into me as tremor after tremor convulsed through her body. After a few moments, she let out a final shudder and her body went limp.

My own body was burning, and my cock was throbbing for release, but I let myself savor the sensation of tasting her passion. Feeling her come on my tongue had only been the start of it, but her sounds and trembling would be forever etched in my memory.

I slowly slid her from my shoulders until I was holding her with her legs circling my waist. Her breathing was ragged as she met my gaze, dark desire hooding her eyes. "Please, Kaos."

CHAPTER
TWENTY-SIX

Kensie

I buzzed with contentment as the Taori held me. It had been so long since I'd experienced that powerful of a release that my body still trembled.

"Please, what?" he asked, in response to my plea.

"I need you inside me," I begged.

I leaned back so that my spine brushed the wall of casks, breathing in the cool air. Despite the temperature of the Vandar ship and the even cooler air inside the storage room, my body felt like it was on fire.

He'd been right. First I would beg him to fuck me. I shivered at that thought, despite my heat. His body was slippery with the sweat that was rolling off him, and he was panting as his body vibrated, as if he was barely restraining himself. For a moment, I wondered if I was making a huge mistake. It was one thing to want a night of passion or to forget everything with some fun, but I was about to fuck a massive, horned alien in the throes of mating fever.

I didn't have any clue what that really meant. Would he rut me like an a out-of-control beast? Would he have incredible stamina? Would I be able to withstand him? I was so much smaller than him, and I'd never been with a huge alien before. Even though I'd been an attendant to the alien fighters in the arena, I'd managed to avoid fucking any of them. Aside from Mick, and he'd been human, and that had been different.

Panic fluttered in my chest. As much as my body ached to be filled by him, and my orgasm had only piqued my desire, I was terrified that I wasn't going to be able to handle it. As much as I didn't want to disappoint him—I was representing human women, after all—but I didn't want to die trying to cure his mating fever.

Before I could figure out how to tell him I was having second thoughts, Kaos was tugging down his pants and notching his cock at my entrance. Since my legs were spread around his waist, there was little way to pull back as his crown bumped me.

Then my heart stuttered. He had three crowns, each one broader than the one above it, the one at the base of his cock the thickest. I'd gotten a full view of them when he'd stripped down at the pool. Then, I'd been shocked by the fact that he was naked and how much of his skin was covered by ink, but now I wished I'd been bold enough to stare at his cock and really study those crowns.

What kind of aliens had three cockheads? I released my clutch on his horns and dropped my hands to his shoulders in an attempt to lift myself.

Kaos growled. "If you aren't ready for my cock, I can always fuck you with my tail."

My jaw dropped. Some of the other attendants at the

arena had whispered about the aliens with tails, but I hadn't heard them talk about this—or maybe I hadn't been listening closely enough. I shook my head quickly. Somehow the idea of tail-fucking was even more startling than a cock with three heads.

"No, I'm ready."

Kaos held my gaze as his hands went to my hips, slipping from the sweat on his palms. "I will go slow for you."

This time, he was the one who captured my lips in a hard kiss. His surprisingly soft lips were familiar to me now, and I moaned into his mouth as he moved my body down onto his thick shaft. I could feel his crown spreading me and then the second one stretching me even more. I dug my fingers into the flesh on his shoulders. Even slow, he felt enormous, and I didn't know how I could take the largest of his heads without breaking in two.

Kaos was dragging in desperate breaths, the strain of having to go slow looking like it might shatter him. His brow was furrowed, beads of sweat popping up around his temples and trickling into his hair.

I shifted my hands back to his horns, squeezing them. "Don't go slow. I can take it."

He hesitated for a beat, but I stroked the ridges on his horns, and he threw back his head and roared as he slammed me down onto his cock.

All the breath in my body left me and stars exploded in front of my eyes. I was glad I was holding onto his horns so I could squeeze them in response to the shock. Kaos held himself inside me as I adjusted to his girth, but his head was still tipped back and his breathing uneven.

Using his horns for leverage, I started moving myself up and down on his cock, just a bit at first. Kaos rolled his head back to face me, his jaw clenched.

"You're so tight," he managed to grit out. "Like the most exquisite vise."

I couldn't speak. It took all my concentration to work myself up and down his rigid length, the sensation of his crowns stroking my inner walls sending shockwaves through me.

Kaos slid his hands up my back. "If I'd known there was a female in the universe who felt like this, I would have insisted my sky ship abandon our mission and search for you."

I found my rhythm, moving my fingers along his striped horns as I bounced up and down. The rough sounds coming from his throat rumbled my bones.

"You're so good at riding my cock, and you take me so well."

I arched my back, sighing as he captured one of my peaked nipples in his mouth. His hot tongue swirled around it before moving to the next one, and then his hands were on my hips again, moving me faster.

I lifted my head and released his horns as his thrusting became frenzied. The sound of skin slapping against skin echoed off the casks and meshed with our moans.

Then, so quickly that I barely registered it was happening, Kaos lifted me off his cock and flipped me over. My arms flailed but grasped the edge of one of the standing casks as he stroked into me from behind and held my legs up.

The new angle felt even deeper, and I gasped for breath as he pounded into me. Craning my head behind me, I could see that Kaos was moving in a barely controlled frenzy. His hair was hanging in his face and sweat glistened on his bare skin.

I dropped my head between my shoulders, my fingers going white as I squeezed the edge of the cask. When the tip of his tail moved between my legs, working its way to caress my clit, I couldn't do anything to stop the release that barreled through me. My body jerked, and I spasmed around Kaos' cock as wave after wave of pleasure slammed into me.

I'd barely stopped quivering when Kaos pulled out, spun me around again, hoisted me onto the top of the cask, and thrust into me a few more times before he bellowed as he pulsed hot into me. He was holding himself deep as he curled his body around mine when the door opened. Light streamed in from the corridor, silhouetting a Vandar warrior as he stood frozen in place.

Kaos didn't move anything but his head, twisting to meet his open-mouthed gaze. "Tell Raas Ronnan that I found my missing mate."

CHAPTER TWENTY-SEVEN

Kaos

The Vandar opened and closed his mouth a few times, reminding me of a Lavarian giggle fish, before staggering from the room and letting the door close behind him.

"So much for staying hidden," Kensie said, swiveling her head around to grin at me.

The heat from my skin was fading and my heart slowed its erratic beat. Then my cock thickened even more, the base crown swelling and locking me inside her.

Her eyes popped wide, and she dropped her gaze. "You're still…? You can still…? You're not done?"

"I don't know if I'll ever be done with you," I told her, the truth of the words hitting me hard. "But I didn't do that to keep fucking you, although I would like nothing less. This is the mating clench."

She stilled. "The what?"

As much as I'd talked about the Quaibyn, I hadn't mentioned one of the crucial elements of it. "The mating clench comes after release. It locks our bodies together until the Quaibyn is fully burned off."

She blinked at me rapidly, and then shook her head as if she couldn't quite understand me. Then she wiggled her hips but flinched when she tried to pull away and couldn't. "We're stuck together?"

"Until my cock unlocks from you, yes."

She cut her gaze to the door. "For how long?"

I twitched one shoulder. "There isn't a set time."

She huffed out an impatient sigh. "Are we going to have to walk around like this for days?"

I couldn't stifle my laugh. "Not that long, although days on some planets are much shorter than others. Maybe as much as a day on a planet with a rapid cycle."

She narrowed her eyes at me, not amused by my hedging. "You could have mentioned this before."

"I wasn't in my right mind before." I shifted my cock inside her and then leaned down to murmur into her ear. "Would you have said no if you'd known you would be filled with me like this?"

She released a breath, her hard nipples brushing my chest. "I didn't say that."

I breathed in the scent of her skin, her sweat mingled with mine. "Explain to me how a human is so perfect for a Taori. By the looks of you, you should not be able to take me as well as you do."

She wrapped one arm around my neck, playing with my hair and winding her fingers to one of my horns. Her fingertips expertly stroked my ridges, sending bursts of pleasure down my spine. "If you explain to me how you know the perfect way to lick me. I know not every alien female has a clit."

I pulled back slightly and cocked my head at her. "Is that what you call that magical little nub that made your heart race and your moans so desperate."

She swatted my chest playfully. "I didn't sound desperate."

"Your moans made me desperate to fuck you, but not until I'd had my fill of your clit." I sat up fully and pulled her ass to the edge of the wooden cask so that her arms could hook around my waist. "I have never encountered another alien female with such wonderful little nubs, but I merely followed your body's lead to bring you pleasure."

Kensie curled her arms around my back and let her cheek rest of my chest. "I might have to keep you."

My heart lurched in my chest. First, I thought it was the usual fear that appeared anytime I thought about risking my heart again, but then I realized that it was relief. I was relieved that she didn't want to run screaming from me, or say that it was a fun, one-time thing. Then I felt something bloom in my chest that had been absent for so long it took me a moment to recognize it. Happiness.

I was happy. Even though I was in an alien ship, unsure if the Vandar were truly allies to be trusted, and hiding in a storage room naked, I was happy for the first time since I'd left Taor.

"The mating clench ensures that you have to keep me," I reminded her.

She laughed and the sound vibrated my chest. "Don't threaten me with a good time." Then she pulled back and peered at me. "I guess when we're locked together, we can't move enough to do anything."

I saw her eyebrows lifting suggestively. Whenever I'd experienced the Quaibyn before I'd been with Quaibyn priestesses on Taor who were specifically trained to attend to the mating fever or with pleasurers who had been thoroughly briefed on the requirements. In those cases, we'd used the mating clench to sleep, but I didn't want to suggest that now. "There are always things to do."

I lifted her, moved us behind the standing casks, then lowered us both to the floor. I stayed on my knees while I let her lie on her back with her legs around my waist. I took her legs and held them wide, staring down at the place where I split her. The thickness of my base crown spread her wide, and the sight sent a possessive thrill through me.

I let my gaze drift to her flushed folds, and I dragged one finger through her, finding her clit again. She twitched when I touched it, and when I glanced up her eyes were flashing heat.

I started swirling the tip of my finger over her clit, and her eyes fluttered closed.

"Eyes on me, Kensie," I said forcefully.

Her eyes flew open.

"Whose cock is inside you?" I asked, circling her clit a little faster.

Her pupils flared as her breathing became rapid. "Yours."

I slowed the pace of my finger. "Who does this perfect little pussy belong to?"

She nibbled the corner of her bottom lip. "It's yours, Kaos."

I growled, eyeing the sight of my cock filling her and her legs spread wide for me. I swirled faster and was rewarded by a breathy moan. "That's right. You're locked to me, Kensie. You're at the mercy of my cock, aren't you?"

She nodded, twitching her hips as I circled faster.

"And you're going to come for me again, aren't you?"

She groaned and arched her back, bobbing her head up and down.

"You're going to come for me again and again, just like

you're going to fuck me again and again," I purred. "Anytime I want this pussy, you're going to spread your legs for me and give it to me, aren't you, mate?"

"Yes, oh, fuck, yes," she murmured.

"Because you're mine, aren't you, Kensie? Every part of you belongs to me now, doesn't it? Especially this perfect, tight pussy that's clenching my cock so tightly."

She nodded as I vibrated my finger on her clit, her eyes rolling back in her head.

"Say it, Kensie," I commanded, needing desperately to hear her say the words. "Say that you're mine."

"I'm yours. Only yours." Her body started to jerk as her release trembled through her, the low gasps slipping from her lips as if they were escaping from the depths of her soul. When she'd sagged to the floor, her eyelids fluttering, I slipped my hands under her back and lifted her into an embrace.

"I will hold you to that promise," I whispered.

She made some soft, incomprehensible sound in my arms that was drowned out by the sudden jolt of the ship. For the briefest moment, I wondered if we were engaged in battle already, but the sound wasn't that of an attack. It was the unmistakable sound of a ship locking on.

CHAPTER TWENTY-EIGHT

Kensie

The distinct sensation of being released by his body was more of a shock than the sharp sounds that rattled the ship. I was no longer anchored to him by the mating clench, and instead of being relieved, I experienced a strange pang of loss. Being locked to the Taori had been intense, but it had also been the most connected I'd been to anyone in longer than I could remember.

Kaos's eyes held mine as we both dragged in deep breaths, the heat in them fading as the sweat cooled on our skin. The moment felt heavy, and I wondered what I should say after just fucking an alien with mating fever and being bound to his body in the most primal way.

"We're being boarded."

I blinked at him, the euphoric daze still muddling my mind. "What?"

Kaos extracted himself from me and stood, pulling me up with him. "The Vandar ship is being boarded. We should go."

A flutter of panic trilled in my chest as I scrambled to wrap my towel around me. "How do you know that? Shouldn't sirens be sounding?"

Kaos shook his head. "If I'm not mistaken, the boarding is planned. My Taori brothers are locking their ship onto this one. If it were an enemy incursion, we should hear sirens—and running warriors."

I cut my gaze to the hallway, which was not flooded by the sounds of thundering Vandar.

"We should meet them." Kaos readjusted his pants and turned toward the door, then looked back at me. "After we find you some clothes."

I released a sigh, grateful that he remembered why I'd ended up down here in the first place. "I'd rather not meet your Taori crew mates in this."

Kaos grunted, his gaze sweeping across me and arousal flickering behind it. "It might be difficult to explain." He held up a finger. "Wait here."

Before I could protest, he'd slipped from the room and left me alone. I huffed out a breath, annoyed that he was back to his sparse communication. He hadn't had any issues talking when he was inside me, although his conversation had consisted of mostly commands then, too.

"Bossy bastard," I grumbled, as I shifted from one bare foot to the other.

Now that I wasn't panting for breath, the cool air made my skin prickle, and the hard floor was like ice. I still didn't know how the Vandar and Taori could be comfortable going shirtless, but neither alien species seemed affected by the cold in the least.

Just as I was considering venturing out on my own, the

door opened and Kaos returned holding out a white swath of fabric. "This should cover you."

"Where did you—?" I started to ask as I took the garment and unfurled it to reveal an oversized tunic. Unless the Vandar liked to put on more clothes to relax, it didn't come from them. "Never mind, I don't want to know where you got it."

Kaos gave me a curious grin. "You have a very suspicious mind for a female. I got it from one of the cooks. They cannot cook without wearing full coverings."

That made sense. I dropped the towel onto the top of the nearest wine cask and pulled the fabric over my head, glad that our alien hosts were so huge it meant the tunic hung far enough down my thighs it could be a dress.

Kaos looked me up and down, his gaze lingering on my curves. "Better." He stepped closer and rested a hand on my hip, rubbing his thumb through the fabric. "You look much better in that than the Vandar I took it off."

My pulse quickened but I was distracted by the thought that there was a shirtless Vandar cook and confused as to whether he volunteered his top or it was taken by force. Knowing how Kaos operated, I wouldn't have been surprised either way.

Kaos growled, his hand sliding to the small of my back and jerking my body flush to his. "As much as I would like to remove this garment from you and see how good it looks in a pile at your feet, we should go."

As swiftly as he'd pulled me to him, he released me and grabbed my hand. I followed him from the storage room, giving a final glance backward at the place where our bodies had been entwined and where I'd succumbed to his primal need to burn off his mating fever. Part of me wished we could stay in that small storage room lined with wooden casks and heavy with the scent of wine and ale. For just that moment in time, there had been nothing but us. No ghosts from the past. No urge to shield my heart.

I was snapped back to the cold reality of the Vandar ship and the impending battle as Kaos rushed us through the warbird. He kept a tight hold on my hand, but I couldn't help worry that the closer we got to being reunited with his crew, the farther away that moment of perfect contentment was slipping.

Then I reminded myself of his urgent words and how he'd ordered me to say that I belonged to him. He wouldn't have said that if he wanted nothing from me, would he? He wouldn't say he was holding me to my promise of being only his if he cared for nothing but quenching the burning flames of his fever.

My heart kept time with the drumbeat of our rapid footsteps as we raced deeper into the Vandar ship and followed the loud clangs and jolts that came from the other side of the vessel. We weren't the only ones following the noise. Many bare-chested Vandar raiders joined us as we drew closer, several stealing curious glances at me, although none dared look for more than a second when they saw Kaos' hand clamped over mine.

I recognized Raas Ronnan at the large docking bay. His legs were set wide, his arms were folded over his chest, and his white-blond hair cascaded down his back as he waited for the ship to complete the locking procedure and the massive circular door to swing open.

When Kaos walked up to him, he glanced over. "You found her."

"I did."

Neither alien said more but I sensed a current of unspoken emotion beneath their words.

"And you found clothes for her?"

Kaos grunted. "A generous donation from one of your cooks."

Ronnan returned the grunt. "Am I to assume there is no need to sequester you?"

Kaos stared forward as the Vandar warlord eyed him with a blend of challenge and amusement. "There is not."

Ronnan didn't get the chance to comment on that as the heavy mechanism on the locking door sprung free and it was tugged open. Kaos' grip on my hand tightened for a moment before the unforgettable figure of Kalesh Naz strode from the attached ship, his steel mesh sash slung across his chest. Kaos released my hand as he rushed forward to greet his kalesh, both men clasping the tops of the opposing shoulders.

I twitched my fingers, which were suddenly cool from the loss of the Taori's warm hand, and I watched the reunion with a twinge of longing. That longing was obliterated when a shriek made me jump.

"Kensie!" Bobbie barreled past the Taori and flung herself at me. "We thought you were dead, then we thought you'd been taken back into the arena, and then we thought..." Her voice cracked as she pulled back and held me at arm's length to size me up. Then she slid her gaze to Kaos and gave me a big grin. "But now I think we might have rescued you too soon."

CHAPTER TWENTY-NINE

Kaos

It was hard to pull my hand from Naz's shoulder. A part of me wanted to be sure it was really him. Ever since I'd heard his voice through the darkness in the alien dungeon, the truth of Kalesh Naz being alive had seemed like a dream.

He'd insisted on being the last one in the escape pods and our sky ship had exploded moments after I'd ejected. Despite believing his assurances that we would meet again and that the story of the sky clan of the Taori did not end there, I'd thought it too much to hope that he'd survived. Then when I'd heard him whisper the battle litany in the dank, hopeless dungeon, I'd been sure the fever was making me hallucinate. But it had been Kalesh Naz then, and it was him now.

"It is good to be reunited with my first officer," he said gruffly. "Again."

I nodded, grasping his shoulder as if he was my anchor. I was vaguely aware of some of the females from the arena rushing to Kensie, but a deep bellow drew my attention.

"Kaos!"

I wrenched my gaze from Naz as other Taori officers rushed toward me. "Daiken?"

The pilot whom I'd last seen so sick with the Quaibyn that I'd been sure he wouldn't survive gave me a broad smile as he threw his arms around me. I was startled by the show of emotion but then Skard piled on, wrapping his massive arms around both of us.

"We heard we almost lost you to the battle moon," Daiken said, when he finally released me.

"It wasn't as treacherous as the forest on Denber Prime," I told him, gaining a belly laugh from Skard.

"You mean the acid forest where everything we touched burned?" Our navigator shook his head. "That's not much of a recommendation."

"If we're reviewing alien moons, I do not recommend the hunting moon." Daiken scowled. "Although I think I'd take running from the Xulonians over having to fight other alien captives."

"All of the moons are twisted and cruel," Kalesh Naz said with such force that I almost stepped back. "Which is why we're going to destroy their ability to subject anyone else to their malevolent desires."

"Things are going according to plan?" Raas Ronnan asked without stepping forward.

Everyone turned to him as Kalesh Naz gave the alien warlord a nod that could have passed for a brief bow. "They are. You have my eternal gratitude for retrieving my first officer and the human female."

Ronnan returned the nod. "We are allies in this fight. All Vandar fight against the subjugation of innocents."

"You were able to eliminate the threat on the battle moon?" Naz asked.

"The arena has been destroyed and all the Xulonians' captives have been rescued." The Vandar twitched one shoulder. "The remaining guards and Xulonians in the arena are unlikely to have survived."

"Good."

I turned to the blonde female who said this. I remembered her from the arena, but now she didn't have a collar around her neck, and she was dressed in pants and a dark top instead of a flimsy dress. She stood beside Kensie with her arm around her waist and her eyes flashing with anger.

"If I'm supposed to feel any kind of sympathy for those assholes because they didn't kill or torture me outright, I don't. They made me watch fighter after fighter get slaughtered." She cut a quick glance to Kensie. "At least I didn't fall for any of them, but not everyone was so lucky."

I noticed Kensie's cheeks flush and the story she'd told me about caring for one of her fighters rushed back to me. I hadn't thought of it since she'd mentioned it but now sent jealousy curling wicked fingers around my heart. How attached had she been to him? Did she still mourn him?

I knew I had no right to the powerful possessive claim I felt to Kensie, but the thought of her with someone else made my heart race and my stomach twist, even if that person was long gone. Did that make me crazy? Maybe the delirium of the Quaibyn hadn't fully released me from its clutches, because I'd never needed to possess any of the other females I'd been with during my past fevers.

Kensie was different. I'd known that since the moment I'd touched her. It was why I'd made her promise herself to me. I shouldn't hold her to the words she'd uttered when we'd been delirious with passion but the need for her to be mine was visceral. She *was* mine.

"They will pay," Kalesh Naz assured the female next to Kensie.

I tried to catch Kenzie's gaze, but she was being pulled into another hug by the pink-haired female that Naz had taken for a mate, who'd rushed onto the ship along with a tall, dark-haired female who looked like she would have been a valiant opponent in the arena.

"You didn't think we'd leave you behind, did you?" Tyrria asked Kensie with a laugh.

I couldn't help sneaking a look at the female's hand, since I knew she had the ability to morph into alien creatures at will and the last time she'd changed, she'd assumed the form of a creature with poisonous hands.

As if sensing my thoughts—or Kenzie's—she held up her hands. "Back to normal. See?"

Bobbie jutted out her bottom lip. "And before you ask, she won't change into any creature you ask her to just for fun."

Tyrria rolled her eyes. "I'm saving my powers for when I need them."

The tall female with dark, curly hair put a hand to the blaster on her waist. "We're all going to get to show the Xulonians what we've got soon enough."

Skard met her gaze and let out a hungry rumble. "If you battle with as much passion as you—"

"Let's save it for the fight," Bobbie said, holding up her palms. "Or at least your private quarters."

So Skard and the imposing female were lovers? Had they met on one of the moons? The female had not been in the arena. That much I knew.

"We had requisitioned another Xulonian ship," Kalesh Naz

said, focusing on Ronnan, but raising his voice so we could all hear. "My warriors and I will join you and Kaos while the females will stay on a ship away from danger."

The female Skard had clearly claimed as his cleared her throat. "Not all the females."

"Carly can join the fight with us," Naz said, "if Lia agrees to protect the females."

Carly gave a curt nod. "Lia won't be happy to be separated from Torst, but she'll do it. She wants to stay close to Val, anyway."

"Torst is alive?" I managed to say, my mind spinning with so many new names.

"We both landed on the hunting moon," Daiken said. "Along with Lia and Val, both from a human freighter taken by the Hettite slavers. Val is the reason I'm alive."

"And Lia is the reason Torst isn't wandering around mad in a subterranean tunnel," Skard added.

Daiken thumped a hand on my back. "I know it's a lot, but I'll explain everything."

"Actually, you won't." Skard nudged the pilot. "That ship filled with females won't fly itself."

Daiken gave me a crooked grin. "I guess I'd better return to my mate and the ship filled with beautiful females." He inclined his head to Kalesh Naz and Raas Ronnan. "You know how to find me."

A part of me wanted to join him because he would be on the ship with Kensie, but I knew my place was by the side of my kalesh.

"You and your warriors are welcome, Kalesh Naz." The Vandar warlord motioned with his head for Naz to join him. "Should we discuss the battle plans in my strategy room?"

Naz moved forward, along with Skard and Carly. I hesitated as Tyrria pulled Kensie with her toward the other ship. I wanted to say something before we were parted, but what could I say in front of everyone? What did I want to say? That I'd meant what I'd said to her? That I knew she was mine in the core of my soul?

Instead, I inclined my head at her. "I look forward to seeing you after the battle."

She opened and closed her mouth but was pulled away by the chattering females before she could respond. Then the doors connecting our ships were sealed with a resounding slam.

CHAPTER THIRTY

Kensie

The steel reverberated as the door connecting our two ships clanged shut. Even though the sound of the other females talking and laughing was loud, the finality of that sound made me flinch.

Bobbie wrapped her arms around me again as we walked through the conscripted Xulonian ship. "I still can't believe we got you back. You know, we didn't even know you hadn't made it onto the ship until we'd left the moon. We were all the way in space when we realized we couldn't find you or the Taori first officer."

"It was chaos." Tyrria looped an arm with mine on the other side. "I was sure I'd seen you on the entrance ramp, but we searched everywhere, and you and Kaos were gone. Naz was not happy. He said we had to go back for you right away."

Bobbie nodded. "He was scary angry. But then we were

hailed by the Vandar, and they offered to get you using their invisible shielding."

The pink-haired, half-Kayling, half-Lycithian nibbled the corner of her bottom lip. "The Vandar rescue went well, right? They treated you and Kaos well?"

I took a breath when both women stopped talking in rapid-fire. "They treated us well." I didn't mention how the warlord had eyed me before Kaos had arrived, or my bafflement at why the Vandar were so eager to join someone else's fight. My knowledge of the Vandar wasn't vast, and it didn't include this platinum-haired horde that was returning and spoiling for a fight.

"Well, I'm glad you're back with us." Bobbie squeezed my arm. "Those Vandar might be hot—and you know I have a weakness for blonds—but I'd rather be here with all the women."

"Not all women," Daiken growled as he passed us on the way to the cockpit.

"Don't let him scare you," Bobbie whispered. "He might look scary but he's a pussycat when he's around Val."

"Who's Val?" My head was starting to spin with all the names I'd heard. Was I supposed to remember all the new Taori and all the females who appeared to be their mates?

"She's the genius who's going to get the Taori back to their own time," a voice said from behind us.

I turned to see a pretty human with long, dark hair pulled into a high ponytail and slightly upturned eyes. She gave me a wide smile and held out her hand. "I'm Lia. Val and I were on the same imperial transport and ended up stranded on the same Xulonian moon."

I took her hand and shook it, taking in her imperial uniform. "So, you're imperial soldiers?"

Her smile faltered. "I am. I was. I was security for the transport that was ambushed. So was Carly." She jerked a thumb behind her. "She went with Skard to fight with the Vandar and other Taori."

I nodded. The woman who'd been eager to join the fighting looked very much the part of a security officer.

"Val was part of the group of scientists we were transporting. She's actually a physicist who specializes in temporal mechanics." Lia's smile brightened. "Like I said, genius. You'll probably meet her later. She's requisitioned the med bay for her work and only emerges to eat and occasionally sleep."

Now that we'd stopped walking to talk to Lia, I took a moment to take in the ship. Unlike the Vandar ship, which was like a cavernous labyrinth of steel, this ship was smaller and more compact. The walls were sleek and dark gray, and the ceilings were high, but the passageways were narrow. I thought back to the few Xulonians I'd seen—tall and impossibly thin—and the vessel made sense.

I was glad the air wasn't as cold as on the Vandar ship, and I didn't miss the shouts and thundering footfall echoing loudly around me. This ship didn't have the feel of a war-ship the way the Vandar warbird had, and my shoulders relaxed as I realized that I was finally—hopefully—safe from danger.

"There you are!"

I heard Trisha before I felt her hug me from behind. I twisted to hug her back and saw more of my fellow attendants from the arena behind her.

"Was I the only one who didn't get off the moon in the escape?"

Trisha pulled back from me, her brown eyes glittering. "We were so worried. We thought that you might be punished for what we'd all done." Her eyes instinctively went to my neck, which was no longer ringed by cold steel that could jolt me with an electrical current if I displeased the alien guards.

I brushed my fingers to the old scorch marks on my throat. "No. When I fell out of the escape vessel, Kaos jumped with me, and we landed on the sand. The guards didn't see us, and we were able to escape into the desert."

Trisha brushed a lock of black hair from her eyes. "You went into the desert? But that's a death sentence."

I remembered what I'd heard the guards say about the moon's barren terrain—that it was harsh and uninhabitable. They'd made us feel like we were lucky to be inside the luxurious arena complex instead of being tossed out into the inhospitable desert.

"I'm not going to say it was easy." My mind went to the punishing heat and the tunnels that had turned out to be an actual sand creature. "But Kaos kept us alive until we could be rescued."

Bobbie cocked her head at me. "Is he the guy who helped us escape, and who was panting like a wild animal?"

I nodded.

All the women gaped at me. Trisha eyed me up and down as if she was looking for signs I'd been mauled by him. "And you're okay? He looked like he was about to eat someone when we were leaving the arena."

Tyrria pushed her way back to me. "Kaos is a Taori like Naz. He's one of the good guys. He never would have hurt Kensie." She gave me a quick, questioning glance.

"He definitely didn't hurt me," I said, quickly. "He's the only reason I survived and didn't get dragged back into the arena."

"And if I remember correctly," Bobbie said with a mischievous wink, "he just happens to be incredibly hot. I'd love to run my hands up and down those tattoos of his."

Tyrria rolled her eyes and pulled me forward. "Luckily for Kaos, he's back on the Vandar ship preparing for the attack on the Xulonians. Now, we should let Kensie get some rest." She let her gaze wander to my oversized tunic. "And maybe we can find her some new clothes."

Bobbie scrunched her mouth to one side as she gave me a once-over. "The Vandar don't have much in the way of female clothing, I take it?"

"Not unless I wanted to wear a leather kilt and nothing else."

"I'm on it," Trisha said. "The Xulonian uniforms usually need some alterations, and I'm good with a needle."

For the first time, it struck me that none of the women were wearing the gossamer dresses from the battle arena. They were all in dark, form-fitting uniforms that actually looked pretty comfortable.

"Our fancy dresses weren't practical in space," Bobbie said. "Besides, we aren't attending to anyone anymore."

Trisha frowned. "Those dresses were part of our captivity, and no one wants a reminder of that."

Tyrria gave me a conspiratorial nudge. "We put them out an airlock."

Trisha tugged me forward. "Let's get you changed, and then we want to hear all about your time on the moon."

The women dispersed, disappearing down hallways and behind sliding doors. I released a breath when it was just me and Trisha. She led me down a skinny corridor, stopping to retrieve a garment from an inset cabinet in the wall.

"It's good to have you back," she said, pausing again in front of a door and waiting for it to glide open. "Our group wasn't the same without you."

My throat tightened. Even though we'd been thrown together in a bizarre situation, the other women working in the alien arena had become like a family to me. We'd been through so much, it was hard to imagine never seeing them again. "I missed all of you too."

She unfurled the dark fabric and held it up to me, her gaze scrutinizing my face. "I'm not sure how it's possible or what happened on that moon, but you look happier right now than you ever did before—and sadder."

I thought of Kaos and how right it had felt to be with him. Then I remembered how easily he'd walked away from me. I swallowed the lump in my throat. "I'm just happy to be with you all again. That's all."

I hoped if I repeated that enough to myself, it would be true.

CHAPTER THIRTY-ONE

Kaos

Skard fell back to walk beside me as we proceeded through the Vandar warbird toward the command deck. "It is good to see you, brother."

I cut my eyes to the navigator and then to the tall, broad-shouldered human walking in front of us. "You as well. Should I ask about your journey?"

"My pod landed in the sea of the lust moon." He lowered his voice so that it was barely audible over the pounding of boots on iron stairs. "I didn't discover it was the lust moon until I swam to the nearest land, which was an island."

My mind whirred with questions, the main one being why I couldn't have crashed there, instead of on a scorching sand moon set up for battling to the death?

"I met Carly there." He inclined his head to the female. "But she'd been brought to the moon on purpose by Hettite slavers, and she was not happy about it. She's a fierce fighter and a valiant opponent."

I stole a glance at him, stunned by the look of pride and affection on his face. "So, you are now mates?"

He gave a curt nod. "It was not an easy road—and the twisted alien games on the lust moon were as much of a confusion as a help—but we eventually realized that we were meant to be together."

I wanted to ask him about the alien games, but he spoke before I could.

"And what of you? You were with a human female on the battle moon until the Vandar rescued you, and you were with her when we boarded this ship."

"Kensie," I said, her name almost painful to utter. "She was one of the attendants for the battle moon, but I did not know her until we were stranded on the moon together."

"She is...?" His open-ended question dangled between us.

What was she to me? Not long ago, we'd been as close as a male and female could be, and she'd been bound to me in the mating clench. But the feelings that had rushed over me hot and intense had been fleeting. One moment I'd been determined that she was mine and would have ripped off the head of any creature who'd stepped between us. The next moment, reality had crept in, duty had taken over, and she'd left for the other ship while I'd remained behind to fight with my kalesh.

"A female I kept safe and away from the battle arena," I finally said.

Skard's expression was solemn. "Our kalesh told us about the battle arena and the dungeons where you were reunited. The Xulonians have no depths when it comes to their craven desires."

"I was not forced to fight like Naz was, so I cannot speak to the horrors of the arena, but the dungeons were bad enough."

Skard put a hand on my shoulder. "You are safe now, brother. We both are." He leaned in close. "And we're going to make the Xulonians pay for what they did to us and all the creatures they have subjugated and tortured."

The strange sadness I'd felt over Kenzie's departure was quickly replaced by a quickening of my pulse. I'd always relied on battle to fill the emptiness. Joining the mission to fight the Sythians had given me purpose when my heart had been broken. Punishing the Xulonians would do the same for me now.

Our group paused at the wide doors to the Vandar command deck before they slid open. Raas Ronnan led the way as his raiders turned sharply and clicked their heels at his arrival.

"The Taori and humans," he flicked a glance at Carly, who bared her teeth in a ferocious smile, "are joining our horde for the attack on the Xulonians. I expect you to treat their leader, Kalesh Naz, with the same respect you treat me, and embrace the Taori warriors as if they were Vandar raiders."

The flaxen-haired warriors grunted their agreement and squared their shoulders. We nodded brusquely in return and followed the warlord into his attached strategy room.

"Now that the females are safe," Kalesh Naz said once the door behind us slid shut, "we can talk about our battle plan."

Ronnan walked to the other side of his desk and braced his palms flat on the surface. "My horde has the advantage of flying unseen."

Naz clasped his hands behind his back. "And the Xulonian ships we have commandeered have the advantage of appearing to be their own vessels."

"They will never see the attack coming," Skard said.

Our kalesh frowned. "They cannot be unaware of the revolts on their pleasure moons. Our only advantage in that is the destruction of the communications on the moons has made it difficult for them to know the full extent of the damage."

"They know that we are on their moons." Skard shifted from one foot to the other. "Or that we were."

"No Xulonians escaped the lust moon to tell what they knew," the female said as she lifted her chin slightly. "But we don't know what they might have told those on the surface before we took their only ship."

"Then we do not have the element of surprise." Raas Ronnan looked up at us. "We need to strike quickly, in order to maintain any advantage our ships might give us."

"Agreed." Naz's voice was a low rumble. "Kaos?"

He hadn't spoken to me for more than a moment when they first boarded the ship, and I noticed his gaze darting to me before he said my name.

"Yes, kalesh?"

"You have not given your opinion, which is unusual." The edges of Naz's lips twitched. "Are you ready for imminent battle?"

His question was deeper than it seemed. When he'd last seen me, I'd been on the verge of madness. Now I was calm and steady. He was asking me if I was cured of the Quaibyn and if I could be trusted in a battle.

"I am ready." I slid my gaze to the Vandar warlord, who was also studying me. He was astute enough to notice the sudden change in me, as well. "With the might of the Vandar, we have a chance to destroy the Xulonian's ability to continue their terror."

Naz gave me a single nod before scraping a hand through his silvered hair. "We have two Xulonian ships outfitted for war. One is led by my security chief, Torst, and he has a

Xulonian on board who has chosen to work with us against his own kind."

Ronnan's brows popped high. "Can the traitor be trusted?"

"He almost died helping my pilot and one of the human scientists escape from the hunting moon. Hue had proven his worth and loyalty."

The Vandar inclined his head. "What can he do?"

"He worked on the hunting moon before he became disgusted by his people's actions and fled. He knows the Xulonian security codes and their operating procedures. He has given us valuable intel on their security structures, and how they protect their planet. He's also told us exactly where to attack to do the most damage to their technology without destroying the entire planet."

Skard shot me a look that told me he wouldn't care if we took out the entire planet.

"The other ship is led by my science officer, and it contains many of the Taori who we found in floating escape pods that had never landed. He also has onboard some survivors from the moons who have unusual powers that could be useful if it ever comes to a hand-to-hand battle."

"Ruun is alive?" I couldn't stop my outburst. When I'd last seen the Taori, he'd been on his way to help Daiken—who had been deep in the clutches of the Quaibyn—off the ship.

Naz held my gaze. "He is. We were able to track down many of our crew mates while the Vandar rescued you."

I let out a heavy breath. When I'd awoken in a forsaken moon of sand, I'd been sure that I would never see my Taori brothers again. That fear had been cemented when I'd been dragged from the desert and thrown into a fetid cell as the fever had threatened to consume me. But then I'd heard Naz's voice. Then, just as now, his words had proven that we would not be so easily defeated.

I could not even regret that I was parted from Kensie. Our separation was not the end of us. She was safe while I fought for both vengeance and the future freedom of scores of innocents. Once the Xulonian were defeated, I could see her again. Then maybe I would tell her that she was much more to me than a cure for my fever. I would tell her that I'd meant what I'd said. That she was mine.

I curled my hands into tight fists. But, first, I needed to spill Xulonian blood. First, we fought.

CHAPTER THIRTY-TWO

Kensie

I rubbed my fingers across the smooth fabric of the Xulonian uniform Trisha had altered for me. Luckily, it was stretchy, so it had only needed a little alteration in the hips, but she'd had to hack off a lot of extra fabric at the bottom.

Thinking of the Xulonians and their bony, red faces with deep, sunken, eye sockets made me shudder, so I forced memories of the arena and my alien captors from my mind. Trisha had assured me that the uniforms they'd found stored in the ship's inset cabinets had never been worn before, so at least I didn't have to be haunted by the image of wearing the same uniform as one of the horrid, lanky aliens.

The Xulonians might be abhorrent, but I preferred their military uniforms to the skimpy, gossamer dresses we'd been forced to wear as attendants to the fighters. The form-fitting dark pants and top might not be feminine, but they were comfortable.

I stepped from the quarters that had been assigned to me and glanced both ways down the corridor. Gray walls as far as I could see, with purple ambient lighting in the ceiling that gave the passageway an eerie glow.

I was curious that the aliens had created the arena to be so filled with light and opulence while they clearly preferred more spartan designs. Maybe they'd designed the arena complex to appeal to the captives and keep us happy enough to do their bidding. A sick feeling churned in my gut at the thought of how long I'd been under their control. Then I smiled as I remembered the arena being destroyed by the Vandar, not a shred of remorse tickling the back of my brain at the realization that all the guards who'd shocked my collar and thrown me into the battle ring for sport had perished in the explosion.

"Good riddance," I murmured. "The universe is better off without them."

I only vaguely recalled which way Trisha had brought me, so I picked a direction at random and started walking. The ship wasn't so huge that I could be lost forever, I reasoned, as I made my way past more sleek doors that were flush with the walls.

I turned a corner and stopped short when a door opened, and Lia stepped out.

She blinked at me a few times, eyed my new outfit, and then grinned. "Much better."

"Is that the new girl?"

The voice came from inside the room Lia had emerged from, and it wasn't one I knew.

I peered around Lia into a room that was vastly different from the compact quarters I'd been given. Instead of a platform bed and drawers set into the walls, this room featured an

L-shaped, glossy worktable, surrounded by countertops and clear-fronted cabinets.

A woman with dark, wavy hair pulled into a messy bun grinned at me from a high stool as she bent over papers and devices strewn over the surface in front of her. There was the faint hint of an antiseptic scent that reminded me of every medical bay I'd ever visited.

"This is Val, short for Valeria." Lia waved a hand at the woman. "She's the one who's figuring out a way to return the Taori to their own time."

"The scientist," I said, remembering that I'd been told she'd taken over the ship's medical bay, which explained the smell.

"You can just call me Val. You're the one the Vandar rescued from the battle moon?"

I nodded, my gaze falling to her messy notes and then back to her face, which was dominated by tired eyes. "How's it going? Finding a way back in time, that is."

She leaned her forearms on the table and sighed. "Temporal mechanics is a tricky field. Time travel is possible—and obviously, it happens, otherwise the Taori wouldn't have been sucked through a temporal wormhole—but it's ducking hard to control."

"Ducking?"

She huffed out a breath and leveled a finger at the other woman as Lia giggled. "That is all her fault. I used to be able to curse freely, but you get stranded on one hunting moon with someone and suddenly you're talking like each other."

Lia held up her palms. "Don't look at me. I haven't picked up a single Spanish curse word, and I've been hanging around you and Carly."

Val frowned but her mouth twitched. "Fork me. I guess your aversion to cursing is catching." She beckoned me forward with one hand. "Come on in. I'm dying for a break and a decent distraction from equations and theoreticals."

Lia stepped aside to let me pass. "I'm going to check in with Torst. I'll catch you girls later."

Val motioned to the stool across from her. "I've met most of the other women who were on the battle moon with you. How are you handling the change?"

"You mean how am I dealing with not being held captive by the Xulonians?" I almost laughed. "Pretty great, actually."

She nodded but leaned back. "That's good. Even though the change is good, it's still a major shift in what you knew. I know it took me a while to recover after getting off the hunting moon."

A shiver slid down my spine. "You were hunted and survived?" She didn't look tough enough to keep from being hunted to extinction.

"I only survived because of Lia at first, and then because of Daiken, Torst, and the other survivors on the moon. We only escaped because we teamed up, which is how we're going to defeat the Xulonians for good."

Her voice had a hard edge of determination. I wanted to feel that same intensity, but she was right. I was still coming to terms with my existence—twisted as it was—being upended. I felt a stab of shame that I knew so little about the other pleasure moons, but a part of me hadn't wanted to know. There had been nothing I could have done, but I still despised myself for living comfortably in the arena complex while this woman had been fighting to stay alive.

I cleared my throat and changed the subject, shifting my gaze back to her work. "Do you think you'll be able to do it?"

She held my gaze for a beat before grinning. "Duck, yeah. We're going to go back in time and return the Taori to their rightful timeline."

"We?" My breath hitched in my chest.

"Sorry. I didn't mean to freak you out. Not everyone, obviously, but I'm returning with them along with Lia, Carly, and Tyrria. Those of us who found Taori we can't imagine living without." She tilted her head at me, her curious gaze narrowing. "What about you?"

"Me?" I spluttered. How could anyone know that Kaos and I were anything to each other? Then my mind stumbled. What were we to each other? Memories of him being inside me made my face heat, but then I thought of how coolly he'd left me on the Vandar ship. Once his mating fever had cooled, had any feelings he'd had for me been doused as well? And could I honestly say I couldn't live without him?

The idea of him traveling five hundred astro-years into the past and never seeing him again made my throat tighten, but so did the idea of going back with him. I knew nothing of the past and his world. At least in this world, I had friends.

"You were with Kalesh Naz's first officer, weren't you?" She gave me what could only be described as a wicked grin. "Any possibility you'd want to travel back in time with him?"

"No," I said more quickly and sharply than I'd intended.

Val jerked back, her pupils widening. "Okay. I was only teasing you since I know from experience what it's like to be stranded on an alien moon with an overheated Taori. I thought—"

"Nope." I managed to give her a tight smile. "Nothing happened between us on the moon." Technically true. "I'm pretty sure the last thing Kaos wants is a frail human like me following him back to his time."

Val shrugged. "If you say so."

CHAPTER THIRTY-THREE

Kaos

I stood shoulder-to-shoulder with Skard on the Vandar command deck, his mate Carly on his other side. Despite him occasionally stealing a glance at her, you wouldn't know that he'd claimed her as a mate, and I admired his ability to keep his warrior's focus.

For the hundredth time, I forced myself to stare at the readouts on the console and make sense of them, and for the hundredth time, my mind wandered away from the data and to Kensie. I bit back a groan. We were on the verge of battle, and all I could think about was the human female.

I gave my head a rough shake, trying to shake off the distraction, as if it were something clinging to me. The last thing I needed was to provide bad information or lead our efforts against the Xulonians astray.

"Are you ill?" Skard said to me in a hushed voice without looking over.

So much for my lack of focus going unnoticed. "I am well."

"If you need more time to recover from being on the desert—"

"I do not need more time," I cut him off. What I needed was to see Kensie again. But what would that accomplish? Was I fooling myself in thinking there was more between us than heat? Despite my confusion, the thought of seeing her again calmed me. Once the battle was over and I could see her again, I would know.

"Incoming transmission from Daiken," Skard said, dropping his concern for me as our console blinked blue.

"Onscreen," Raas Ronan said, from where he stood behind us next to Kalesh Naz. Both leaders had their hands clasped behind their backs and radiated cool command.

The wide view screen flickered, but it wasn't Daiken that filled it. The pretty human female who smiled at us had a mass of curls piled on top of her head and noticeable circles under her eyes.

"Val!" Carly grinned at the woman.

"Sorry to interrupt your battle prep. I was hoping to give a brief update to the Taori on my work."

Naz pivoted to Ronnan. "Permission to transfer the transmission from the screen so the entire command deck isn't disturbed."

Ronnan nodded, flicked his hand at one of his nearby Vandar raiders, and the image of Val disappeared from the enormous view screen and reappeared on the console in front of me.

"Hey again," Carly said with a throaty laugh. "Now you look more realistically sized."

Kalesh Naz jumped from the platform where he'd been standing with the Vandar warlord and joined us. "I trust you have something to report."

Val's expression became more serious. "I do, but there's good news and bad news."

Naz grunted. "I suppose I should be grateful there is good news at all."

"That's the spirit," Val said, her voice lilting. "The good news is that I've figured out how to get you all back in time. The not so good news is that I haven't quite figured out how to pick the time."

"Meaning?" Skard asked.

"Meaning she could send us back two astro-years or a thousand, but she can't be sure which one, right?" Carly said before Val could answer.

"I don't think that's what she meant," Skard grumbled, shooting his mate a look.

"Actually, that's pretty much it." Val gave us an apologetic smile. "The actual moving you through time isn't the tricky part. It's landing on the right time."

"What happens if you send us to the wrong time?" Our kalesh leaned his hands on the console on either side of her image. "Would we be stuck there?"

She shook her head. "There's no indication the trip would be dangerous. If we got the timing off, we could theoretically try until we got it right."

Carly rubbed the back of her neck. "That sounds like a lot of time travel. Are you sure it won't scramble our brains?"

"The temporal wormhole did accelerate our Quaibyn." Skard glanced at Carly again, but this time it was with a wicked half-grin. "So, we know it can have effects on our physiology."

Val folded her arms over her chest and leaned back. "The Quaibyn thing was weird, and it might have been a unique phenomenon—like your mating fever. But we now have a serum to stop the fever, courtesy of the alien spider venom."

I huffed out a breath, remembering hearing about the discovery, but still amazed a substance from a different world could cure our sickness. "I would not want to experience the Quaibyn each time we tried to reach our own time."

Naz and Skard both made their own low sounds of displeasure.

"And if the serum stops working, at least this time, you'll have a ship full of females." Carly elbowed Skard in the ribs. "Some of them actually willing."

"The females are returning to the past with us?" I asked, swiveling my head to glance at Naz and Skard.

"Only the ones who have a reason to go," Carly said, sliding her gaze to Skard. "Like me."

"And me," Val piped up from the screen. "Tyrria is also coming with us, obviously." She inclined her head at Kalesh Naz. "And Lia since she's with Torst."

"None of the other females?" My voice cracked as I asked.

Val shook her head. "Most of them want to stay in their own time. It's what they know. Besides, the women who were captives on the battle moon became a tight-knit group. Tyrria is the only one coming, but she doesn't really count since she wasn't in the arena for long."

"And she was on our ship before she was stranded on that moon," Carly said. "If anything, she's one of us."

"What about your friend from the lust moon?" Val asked Carly. "Do you think she'll come with us?"

Carly shrugged. "Like you said, it's a lot to ask someone to go back in time five hundred astro-years."

My stomach had hardened into a knot. If Tyrria was the

only one of the female attendants who wanted to come back in time with the Taori, that meant that Kensie didn't. But Carly was right. It was a lot to ask someone to leave their life and their time behind. I had no right to ask, or even hope, for a female I barely knew to make that kind of sacrifice.

"Thank you for the update, Valeria," Kalesh Naz said, the deep burr of his voice bringing me back to the moment.

"My pleasure." She visibly stifled a yawn.

"Go get some sleep, *chica*," Carly said, dropping her voice. "You look exhausted."

Val waved her off. "I'll sleep when I'm dead, or when we're five hundred years in the past."

Then she clicked off. Naz let out a breath and returned to his post beside Raas Ronnan.

Once again, I attempted to focus on the battle plans, but my body churned with the old feelings of betrayal. They'd been dormant for a long time, but the ache and humiliation were as familiar as old friends. Or perhaps, old enemies.

Why should I feel betrayed by Kensie? She'd made no promises I hadn't forced her to in the heat of passion. She'd never given me any indication she was looking for a mate. A few moments of joy and pleasure, maybe, but nothing so serious and committed that it would require her to abandon everyone and everything she knew and follow me five hundred astro-years into the past.

I was being foolish to expect anything more from her. Would I give up my Taori mission and brothers to be with a female I'd just met? The question stopped me. But she wasn't a female I'd just met. At least, she didn't feel that way to me. Kensie felt like someone I'd known forever. When I touched her, she felt like destiny, and when I'd been inside her, I'd felt complete.

I emitted a deep growl. It didn't matter what I felt. She

wasn't coming. I needed to get used to the idea of losing her—even though the thought of never seeing her again and being separated by half a century stabbed at me like a blade to the gut.

When we went back in time, she would cease to exist. My heart twisted in my chest. Maybe my soul would, too.

CHAPTER THIRTY-FOUR

Kensie

I took a bite of the brown mush, cringing in anticipation of the horrid taste. When the sweetness hit my tongue, I almost jumped with surprise.

"I told you it wasn't bad." The blonde laughed at me, waving the metal ladle, and sending a few globules of food flying. "It might look gross, but I've added enough flavoring to make it edible."

Steam billowed from a tall, metal pot on the small stove, filling the room—which was mostly steel cabinets with cooking utensils lashed to the walls—with a heady, sugary aroma. There was barely enough room for the woman behind the range to move back and forth, but she operated in the tight confines as if she was a seasoned expert.

"Where did you learn to cook...?" I left the end of the question hanging, since I'd forgotten the name the woman had given me when I'd wandered into the galley kitchen.

"Erin." She flipped a curl from her forehead. "Not on the lust moon, that's for sure. Everything was cooked for us there." She sighed then frowned. "Some of it was delicious, but I'll take this stuff any day over having to be there."

I took another bite of the sweet oatmeal-without-oats concoction and shifted my weight from one leg to the other. The texture took some getting used to, but Erin was right. It was flavorful. What flavors I was tasting, I wasn't exactly sure, but it grew on you.

"Once we escaped from the lust moon, I needed to do something to keep me busy. I was part of a resistance fighter group before I was abducted, but there wasn't much need for a spy onboard."

"So, you decided to cook."

She twitched one shoulder. "The Xulonians don't have very sophisticated palates, or maybe they're so developed they've evolved away from the need for food to taste good, but none of the food that was stocked in the ship tasted great. I decided I could dedicate myself to creating decent tasting food out of their highly nutritious and completely tasteless mush."

I gave her an appreciative nod. "I'm glad you did. If it tasted anything like it looked, I wouldn't be nearly as happy to finish this."

She beamed. "It's rewarding to discover a talent I didn't know I had after being in a place where I was only rewarded for one thing."

I didn't press her about her time on the lust moon. The one good thing I could say about being an attendant on the battle moon was that I hadn't actually been expected to perform with the fighters. If I had—and I'd been watched while forced to do it—I don't know if I'd been as upbeat as Erin was.

"How many of you made it off the lust moon?" I scraped my spoon on the bottom of the bowl, shocked I'd almost finished it.

"Only four of us—me, Carly, Ty, and Skard." Her mouth became a thin line. "I honestly don't know how many of the others on the moon were Xulonian avatars, or actual captives like us." She flapped a hand dismissively. "But we got off, and there's no going back."

"Have you considered going back with the Taori?" I asked, even though it wasn't a smooth segue.

She raised an eyebrow. "You mean back with them when they return to their own time?" She shook her head. "As much as it will break my heart to say goodbye to Carly, my life is here. Once we kick the Xulonians to the curb, Ty and I will be returning to the Novaya resistance—whatever's left of it. There's always injustice to fight somewhere."

Now I cocked an eyebrow at her. "Ty?"

Her cheeks flushed. "He's the Neebix who also escaped with us. Turns out, he was a Novaya pilot, but we never met until the lust moon. We might have been thrown into a messed-up situation, but he was always good to me." Her blush deepened. "In more ways than one."

"You're together?"

She nodded. "Once we were away from the twisted manipulations of the lust moon, we were able to realize how much we had in common and connect in more than just the bedroom. Actually, it was a relief to finally sleep together and get some sleep."

I couldn't help laughing at this. I wasn't sure if it was her experience on the lust moon, but Erin didn't seem to have a filter or care what anyone thought of her. I had to admit that I admired her confidence. "I guess that's one good thing to come from your abduction."

"Don't get me wrong." Erin waved the ladle and sent more wet clumps of food flying. Now that I noticed, the shiny steel walls and ceiling were already dotted with dried specks of food. "The Xulonians deserve to be obliterated for what they've done, but a decent number of us have been able to find some good in what happened to us. At least, we met other captives who made it worthwhile."

My thought immediately went to Kaos. I never would have met him if I hadn't been on the battle moon. Tyrria never would have encountered Naz. None of us would have escaped.

Erin dropped the ladle back in the heavy steel pot on the stove and tapped the controls to douse the heat. "If you're done, I'm going to pop out and make a vid call to Ty before everything gets crazy."

"He isn't on this ship?"

She shook her head. "They needed his piloting skills on one of the other commandeered Xulonian ships."

An idea tickled the back of my brain. Instead of pushing it aside or worrying what the women might think of me, I decided to take a page from her book. "Would you mind showing me how to make a vid call?"

Her blue eyes widened. "You want to make a call?"

I nodded. "I should talk to Kaos before the battle. He's the Taori I was stranded with on the moon."

"Oh, I heard." She gave me a knowing smile, then waved for me to follow her. "Come on. Let's do it."

I fell in step behind her, but we only walked a few doors away before Erin was leading me into a room that made the galley look spacious. The walls looked like they were made of computers and there was a single desk with a monitor.

"Communications hub," Erin said. "You could also use the cockpit but that's not so private."

She sat down at the one chair and tapped her fingers

briskly across the smooth surface of the console. "Kaos is on the Vandar ship, right?"

I nodded. "The lead horde ship." I glanced at the door, old feelings of anxiety jangling my nerves. "Are we authorized to do this?"

"It's on an encrypted channel. I do it all the time."

Not exactly an answer to my question, but I guess I was going with it.

"Hailing the ship now."

My stomach did an uneasy flip. Suddenly it hit me that I didn't know what I was going to say. What was my excuse for hailing him while he was preparing for battle?

Before I could tell Erin that this was a horrible idea and we should abort, a Vandar face appeared on the screen. His eyes were dark, but his hair was almost white-blond, although he didn't radiate power like Raas Ronnan did. At least *he* hadn't answered the hail.

"State the purpose of your transmission."

Erin smiled brightly at his stern expression. "My friend here needs to talk to Kaos."

My face burned as the Vandar scowled and then made a dark, disapproving noise. Then he vanished and Kaos appeared in his place. He didn't look any happier to see me.

Erin leapt up and pushed me into the chair, giving a silent wave and darting from the room.

"Kensie?" Kaos narrowed his eyes at me through the screen.

I managed to clear my parched throat and smile. "Hi."

"Is everything all right on the ship?"

"It's fine. It's great." I was babbling. "I wanted to talk to you before the battle."

One of his dark brows arched. "About?"

He was so cool and calm that my earlier exuberance at

seeing him was quickly fading. Not only did he not seem excited to see me, I had a feeling that I was bothering him.

"I wanted to make sure we were okay," I blurted. "Everything happened so fast and then I was leaving the ship and I didn't want you to think..."

My words were coming out all wrong. What I really wanted to do was ask him if he wanted me to come with him, but that question seemed too much of a risk. I'd already taken a chance in contacting him and I got the feeling even that had been a mistake.

"I didn't think anything except that you were reuniting with your friends," Kaos said. "Isn't that what you wanted?"

"Well, yes," I stammered, "but we—"

"We worked well together to survive the moon, and I am grateful for all you did to aid me."

His words were so measured and cold that I felt like I'd been slapped. All I did to aid him? Was that how he was putting it? Embarrassment washed over me, and tears stung the backs of my eyelids.

"Then I guess we should say goodbye," I snapped.

He held my gaze, his own bright-blue eyes somber. "Goodbye, Kensie."

I jammed my fingers on the console to end the transmission so he wouldn't hear the sob welling in my chest or see the tears spilling down my cheeks.

CHAPTER
THIRTY-FIVE

Kaos

I slammed my fist onto the console in frustration. "Spawn of a Sythian!"

One of the Vandar nearest me glanced over, his dark eyes questioning. I wanted to assure him that I wasn't mad with fever or on the verge of losing control. My Quaibyn was no longer a threat, but that didn't mean I was at peace.

My palm tingled, as I almost choked out a laugh at the thought of peace. How could my soul be at peace when I was preparing for war? I glared at the readouts and focused on the information we were quickly compiling about the enemy's planetary security. The access code provided by our Xulonian convert had given us a foot into the alien's systems, and we were accessing their internal operations as well as their weaponry. As promised by the Vandar, their invisible horde had brought us within the orbit of Xulon and the unseen fleet of warbirds was hovering above the unsuspecting aliens preparing to unleash fire and blood.

Despite the impending attack, it wasn't the battle that made my heart pound and my mind skitter like a Velleren water bug. It was Kenzie's expression as I'd told her goodbye.

I'd been caught unawares by her hail. The Vandar who had patched her transmission through to me had made it clear with his glower that personal communications were not customary on warbirds. They were unheard of on Taori sky ships, as well, but that was because we were too far from our home world to receive messages from family, and we didn't make bonds that lingered as we traversed the universe.

At first, I'd worried she was hurt, or their ship was in danger. Then she'd started talking quickly, her chirpy, nervous words drawing attention from others on the command deck. I'd gotten the sinking feeling that she wanted to make sure I hadn't gotten the wrong idea about our encounter. She didn't want me to think...what? That she typically spread her legs for aliens she hadn't known long? That she made it a habit to fuck in storage rooms that smelled of wine and ripe wood?

I'd saved her the embarrassment of saying more and cut her off before she could reveal any details of our time together to the curious warriors around me on the Vandar command deck. I'd thanked her for her help, although a thank you uttered across a transmission seemed lacking, considering the fact that she'd cured me of my raging fever. She'd deserved more heartfelt gratitude, but it was impossible when I was surrounded by other warriors, eager to get to the battle.

She'd cut the call short without me having to tell her I needed to get back to my tasks at hand. At least I hadn't been the one to insist on the goodbye, although her face looked stricken when I bade her farewell.

Goodbye. The word tasted like ash in my mouth. Had I

really said a final goodbye to the female I'd been so sure was mine? It seemed impossible that I'd gone from feeling like I was finally whole to being consumed with a wracking emptiness.

I shook my head. It hadn't been goodbye forever. I was sure to see her after the battle. I tightened my jaw in determination. More reason to fight for victory and revel in the enemy's demise. Once we'd crushed the Xulonians, I could be reunited with Kensie and then I could tell her what I couldn't over the transmission. Which was what?

The question lodged in my throat. I already knew she didn't have any intention of leaving her time or her life here. My destiny was to return with my Taori crew to our time and carry out our mission. There could be no future for us, so what was there to say that wouldn't cause heartache and regret?

"Maybe it's better this way," I muttered to myself. Maybe a clean break was less painful for us both. She was safe. I was going into battle. Afterward, we would both return to lives that didn't include the other. There was nothing else to say.

"What is better?" Skard asked as he walked up to join me.

I straightened my shoulders and grunted. "Nothing. I am honing in on facilities used to run their moons so they can never escape their world again."

"Is that all?"

I cut my eyes to him. If the navigator suspected anything, he had no way of confirming it. As happy as I was for my Taori brothers who'd found mates while on the enemy moons, I did not want them believing that I would share in their good fortune. I did not want their pity when there was no female by my side when we made the journey back to our own time and space. "There is nothing on my mind but cutting down the enemy and making them pay for obliterating our sky ship."

He pounded a hand on my back. "Then let us ride into the

valley of death like our ancestors and drag the Xulonians to the shadowland of demons."

My heart thundered at his words, all thoughts of Kensie forced from my mind as my body tensed for battle. Against all odds, Kalesh Naz had reassembled almost the entirety of our crew, just as he'd promised. We'd gathered allies and commandeered ships. The gods of the ancients had protected us to bring us to this moment. It was the fate of the Immortals to rise from the ashes again and again. Now, we were going to mete out the vengeance that the Xulonians so richly deserved.

"Prepare to launch the attack," Raas Ronnan bellowed from behind us. "Targets locked on their defenses and their power sources."

Skard returned to his post as I quickly locked onto a manufacturing facility that our Xulonian traitor had identified as a place for producing the avatars used on their twisted recreational moons. I knew that the xenophobic aliens didn't actually leave their planet to watch the blood sport on the battle moon, or engage in the deadly hunt on the hunting moon, or even copulate with unsuspecting creatures on the lust moon. They did all this by use of avatars, which they called dimensionals.

I locked in the photon torpedoes with a satisfied grin. They would never be able to enjoy their cowardly fun from afar again.

"Into the valley of death ride the Ten Thousand," Kalesh Naz growled as consoles beeped with the targeting of weapons.

"We are the Taori," I chanted with Skard in response. "We are Immortal."

"Let us show them what the Vandar and Taori can do together," Raas Ronnan roared. "Let them see what Vandar and Taori vengeance feels like."

The command deck rippled with excited energy.

Ronnan pumped his fist into the air. "For Vandar!"

"For Vandar!" his warriors shouted in unison, their own fists thrust high into the air.

A pulse of anticipation arrowed through me, the desire for retribution almost as great as my Quaibyn hunger. The familiar tingle made my cock thicken, but I pushed all memories of Kensie from my brain as I unleashed my weapons on the alien world.

She was safe from the hell I was unleashing. That gave me almost as much gratification as the sight of balls of fire and smoke billowing from the planet's surface as the ship's battle sirens wailed and the command deck was bathed in light as crimson as blood.

CHAPTER THIRTY-SIX

Kensie

I leaned my back against the cool, smooth wall of the corridor. I'd stumbled out of the communications hub once I'd disconnected with Kaos, and I'd waved Erin inside so she could hail her guy before the battle. I'd been grateful she'd been too distracted and eager to talk with Ty to notice my tear-stained face and eyes which were sure to be red.

That had been a while ago, and I'd been walking slowly around the ship ever since. It wasn't anything as huge and cavernous as the Vandar vessel, but it was easy to walk in a circle if you tried. I replayed my conversation with Kaos, but as many times as I went over it in my head, it never got any less painful. He'd been so different from the passionate alien that I'd known on the battle moon—and especially in the storage room—that I couldn't reconcile the hot and cold versions of him in my mind. One thing had been abundantly clear—the

Kaos who was ruled by passion was gone, replaced by one as cold and unyielding as a knife's blade.

"No, thank you," I said, squeezing my eyes closed and moving my head from side to side.

"Are you talking to me?"

I opened my eyes as Tyrria walked toward me, her brow wrinkled.

I forced myself to laugh. "No, I was just thinking aloud."

Tyrria gave me a sympathetic smile. "Are you worried about the battle, too?" She hooked an arm through mine. "I was on my way to the cockpit to see if Daiken has gotten any news yet. Want to join me?"

I should probably have said no. Thinking about the Vandar and Taori fighting against the Xulonians would only make me think of Kaos more, and images of him were what I was trying to purge from my brain. But as much as he'd hurt me, I couldn't stop myself from worrying about him—about all of them. I knew Tyrria was hiding her own anxiety about Naz, but I suspected she had the same ball of fear in her stomach.

"Let's go," I told her, despite my better instincts.

She hugged my arm close to her as she led me through the gray hallways of the alien vessel, each passage—to my eyes—an exact replica as the one before it. No wonder I'd felt like I was walking in circles before. The air wasn't as cool as on the Vandar ship, but it also didn't carry the distinctly masculine scent of a vessel that was packed to the gills with massive, male warriors. Part of me missed the spicy, musky smell that was one-hundred-percent male, while another was glad not to have a further reminder of the Taori.

The hallway we'd walked down emptied into a larger, circular space surrounded by spokes of corridors. Tyrria flicked her fingers through her pink, sideswept bangs as she tugged me down one and into a space that was a cross between a cockpit and a bridge. It wasn't as spacious or impressive as the Vandar command deck, but it held more than a cockpit's usual pilot and copilot seats.

A half-moon-shaped console swept across the front of the space, with three swivel chairs positioned in front of it. A tilted view screen angled toward the console and displayed a view of the inky blackness of space. Behind that were two more stations facing each side, flat screens lining the walls above them.

I recognized the silvery horns of Daiken, who sat in the center of the console. His fingers flew across the glossy, gray surface as Erin perched on the seat to the left of him, her gaze fixed on the images flashing across one of the inset screens.

She glanced back as we entered, giving us both a quick smile before her expression regained its intensity. Gone was the bubbly blonde who'd been in the kitchen. Now I could see the resistance side of her that I'd had a hard time imagining before.

"Any news?" Tyrria asked.

"The Vandar horde initiated the attack," Daiken said, without looking back at us. "They used the element of surprise well. From the reports, it seems like they were able to knock out a decent amount of Xulonian defenses before they knew what was happening and could return fire."

"But they didn't destroy them completely?" Tyrria peered out the front of the ship, as if she would be able to see any of the battle, when, in fact, we were far from the action, and hidden behind one of the moons.

"The enemy has impressive defenses. There was no way to eliminate all of it in the original attack."

"That's the problem with xenophobes," Erin muttered darkly. "Their paranoia makes them have serious weapons of defense."

The nagging ball of worry in my gut churned. "Are the Xulonians returning fire on the horde?"

"The Vandar are flying in something they call the amoeba formation to evade incoming fire, but every time they launch missiles, it opens them to Xulonian attack. So far, no ships have been lost, but a few have been hit."

Fear iced my skin. I wanted to ask if the lead ship had been hit, but I also didn't want to know how much danger Kaos was in.

"The commandeered Xulonian ships filled with our fighters are going in." Daiken's voice was tight. "Let's hope they can provide a distraction so the Vandar horde can disable the Xulonian weapons and end the fight."

Daiken's tone was tense, and I feared he was hiding the truth from us. What if we didn't win? What if our ships were the ones destroyed, and the Xulonians were able to maintain their cruel dominion? What if the only ship of survivors from the moons ended up being ours?

Suddenly, my anger at Kaos seemed petty. How could I have cut off our transmission? What if the last thing I got to say to him was a snippy goodbye?

I wanted to run back to the communications hub and go back in time so I could tell him what I'd been too scared to say before. I didn't want this to be goodbye, and I didn't want to say goodbye when he left with his crew. I wanted to go with him.

Just then, our ship shook so hard I stumbled hard into Tyrria, who hit the wall with a cry.

"What the hell?"

I was about to ask the same thing when I heard a sound I recognized, and one that sent terror slithering down my spine. Another ship was clamping onto ours.

CHAPTER THIRTY-SEVEN

Kaos

"Report!" Raas Ronnan's voice cut through the angry buzz of static and shouts on the command deck.

"The enemy is in retreat, Raas," one of the Vandar raiders yelled over the din. "Our decoy Xulonian ships were able to get close enough to the surface to take out the last of their planetary defenses."

"And the decoy ships with our warriors and allies?" Kalesh Naz asked, his tail swishing behind him as he stood restlessly beside the Vandar warlord.

"No casualties reported, Kalesh." Skard swung his head around to face Naz. "The enemy was not able to return fire in time. Now they don't have the ability to strike—or defend themselves from our attack."

My fingers tingled with the urge to launch every last missile and torpedo remaining in the vessel. It would be so easy to wipe the Xulonians off the map once and for all. They'd done nothing but rain terror on aliens they believed were inferior. Now maybe they should get a taste of what it was like to be helpless and in deadly peril.

"Your orders...?" I hesitated before automatically saying the word 'kalesh.' This was not a Taori ship, and Kalesh Naz was not the one I should ask.

Raas Ronan turned to Kalesh Naz. "What are our orders?"

"The Taori fight to save the universe from suffering. It is not our nature to destroy without provocation."

"You do not think the Xulonians have provoked their own destruction?" I asked, even though I knew the leaders were not talking to me.

Naz pivoted his head to me. "I understand your rage, Kaos. I feel it too. But we should not lower ourselves to the level of those who are soulless."

I clenched my jaw. I would not mind stooping to that level if it meant the evil aliens enjoyed a taste of the bitter poison they'd been doling out to innocents.

"We have destroyed the facilities on all of their pleasure moons," Raas Ronnan said. "We have obliterated their planetary defenses, and their ability to manufacture their dimensionals."

Naz nodded. "The buildings the Xulonian traitor identified as belonging to the collective that operates the pleasure moons have been wiped from the planet. We have severely damaged their power stations, and we have leveled their fleet. They will not be able to subjugate anyone for a very long time."

A very long time didn't seem long enough to me, but I was not the Kalesh or the Raas.

"Make sure these creatures have no ability to leave their planet or attack any ships entering their system," Ronnan added. "I want every Xulonian ship destroyed, and their airbases leveled to ash."

I gave a curt nod and spun back to my console. That was an order I could gladly follow. I scanned the surface of the Xulonian home world, feeling a sick satisfaction at the pock-marked surface and the billowing black smoke rising from craters where buildings once stood. I targeted the last remaining unmanned space vessels perched on vacant flight decks and fired, grinning when the gray hulls exploded in balls of crimson fire.

"Two of our warbirds were hit during the battle, Raas," a Vandar said. "No casualties, but their weapons are offline, and their invisibility shielding is failing."

"Alter the horde's flying formation from the amoeba to the defensive shield pattern until they are fully operational." Ronnan leapt from the raised platform and strode to the nearest standing console. He peered at the readouts. "The horde should be restored quickly."

"Were those our only losses?" Kalesh Naz joined me at my console, his question more pointed to me than to the entire command deck.

Before answering, I ran more scans of the Vandar horde ships then I focused in on the commandeered Xulonian vessels filled with our warriors. "No damage to the ally vessels." Then my eye caught on the flashing blue light. "One is hailing us now."

Before I could accept the hail, it was put onscreen by another warrior. The view of the smoldering planet was replaced by a male with nubby brown horns peeking from within his long golden hair. I knew that the ships weren't filled with only Taori, but I hadn't known that there were Neebix in our ranks.

"Decoy Alpha reporting in," the alien said with a wide grin. "Looks like we did it."

"Ty!" Skard stepped toward the view screen. "Did you get to put your resistance pilot training to the test?"

The Neebix winked, and I remembered the species' reputation. "I haven't had this much fun since the Novaya were chased by the imperial fleet into an exploding asteroid belt."

Skard laughed and his mate, Carly, shook her head. "I'm just glad that Erin wasn't there to witness you taking risks."

"Don't let the human fool you." The Neebix waggled his eyebrows. "She's Novaya resistance through and through and loves risk as much as the next spy."

I wasn't sure what they were talking about, but I guessed that this Neebix had been with Skard on the lust moon.

"Good work infiltrating the planet's security," Skard said. "Your ships slid through their barricade like it was nothing."

Ty shrugged off the compliment but beamed. "Like I said, once a sneaky resistance fighter, always a sneaky resistance fighter."

"Speaking of our other member of the Novaya resistance," Carly said, squinting at her console. "Has the ship of females checked in?"

"I hailed Daiken, but I haven't heard back." Skard frowned at his screen. "Maybe it got diverted in the battle. I'll hail him again."

Unease stirred in my core, although it was foolish to be concerned over one missed hail during a major battle. The ship with the females was hidden far from the fighting. They'd been intentionally kept away from danger.

"No response," Skard said under his breath.

The Neebix's bright smile dimmed as he tapped away on his end. "Their position behind the moon hasn't changed, but they're not alone anymore."

"Impossible," Kalesh Naz growled. "No Xulonian ships escaped from the surface before or during the battle, and we destroyed or stole all the ones on the moons."

Skard raked a hand through his hair and turned to Naz, his expression tortured. "The ship with them is not Xulonian."

CHAPTER THIRTY-EIGHT

Kensie

"We're being boarded." The Taori pilot's voice dripped with dread as he spun around to face us.

"How?" Erin's mouth fell open.

"Ship's sensors didn't pick up their presence until they were on top of us." Daiken cut his gaze to his console. "Literally."

My stomach dropped, as I thought about the other women on board. Would they hear the sounds and know what was happening? "We have to warn the others."

"I can try to seal off the sections of the ship before they reach the quarters." Daiken's fingers danced across the glossy surface of his controls. "Maybe if I cut off life support near the boarding point...?"

Tyrria swept a shaky hand through her hair. "That sounds risky."

"Not as risky as being taken captive." I locked eyes with her. "If this is who I think it is, I'm not going to be taken again."

"Same." Erin nodded fiercely. "I'd rather die fighting."

Tyrria's mouth became a hard line as she squared her shoulders. "Then let's go."

"Wait." Daiken's voice was strangled as he turned back to us, and his expression twisted in pain. "Valeria. She gets so absorbed in her work, she won't notice until..."

Erin rested a hand on his shoulder. "Don't worry. We'll get your girl."

"I'll do what I can from here and then I'll join the fight."

We left him working feverishly and raced from the small bridge. I expected to hear sirens blaring overhead, but there was no sound but our fast footsteps. Daiken was purposefully not sounding the alarm to let the enemy believe they hadn't been detected. That would give us some element of surprise, or perhaps make them overconfident.

I followed Tyrria and Erin, who knew the alien ship better than I did. We dashed through the central hub and then down a corridor.

"Start knocking on doors," Tyrria said in a low voice. "Tell everyone to head to the front of the ship away from where the enemy ship has locked on."

I took one side of the passageway and Erin took the other while Tyrria ran ahead and turned the corner.

I used the flat of my palm to pound on the nearest door, almost relieved it was Bobbie on the other side when it slid open. "Come on. The ship is being boarded." I waved for her to come out of her room. "We have to get to the front of the ship."

"Boarded?" The blonde's cheeks paled. "Fuck me."

"No time for that, girl." Erin said from behind me. "We

need to put as much space as possible between us and them. I, for one, am not being anyone's captive again."

"You and me both." Bobbie joined us and ran to the door next to hers. "Rise and shine, Trisha. Time to run from asshole aliens again."

"What?" Trisha was bleary-eyed when the door glided open. "Is this a joke?"

Bobbie looped her arm through our friend's and tugged her from her quarters. "Would I lie about this?"

Trisha looked at me for confirmation.

I nodded. "Our ship is being boarded. We need to get as far from the incursion as possible."

More women were emerging from the doors along the corridor. I waved them in the direction we'd come from. "Head for the cockpit and stay quiet. We don't want the assholes to know that we know."

"Aren't you coming?" Bobbie asked as she and Trisha hung back from the fleeing women.

"I need to make sure that Val gets out," I told them. "But I'll be right behind you."

I gave them a push before running behind Erin in the opposite direction. "I hope you know where the old med bay is, because this place is a maze to me."

She tapped her temple. "Don't worry. I've got it memorized. We're almost there."

My heart pounded as we rushed down one passageway and then another. Where was Tyrria? The scraping sounds had stopped, which meant that the aliens had probably gotten into our ship, but I didn't hear the sounds of blaster fire. When I'd been on the imperial transport with my family, it had been blaster fire and screaming that had told me something was wrong. Now, there was an eerie quiet.

Had Daiken been successful in trapping the attackers in

one section of the ship? Had he stopped their attack by cutting off life support, or had the cruel abductors learned to be more subtle?

We rounded a corner and Erin tapped the side of a door, which opened silently. Val looked up at us, blinking a few times as if not sure why we were there.

"Grab your notes," Erin ordered in an insistent whisper. "We're being boarded."

The dark-haired woman didn't say a word. Instead, she scooped up her mess of papers in one hand and a tablet in the other and raced around the worktable. "We can't let them get my research."

"I know." Erin pressed her lips together. "That's why we're here."

"Daiken sent us," I added. Somehow I knew Val would feel better knowing that the Taori was thinking about her, even if he wasn't the one who had come to get her.

Val's expression softened for a beat, and I tried not to feel envy at the clear affection between the two. Even though he'd officially said goodbye to me, I ached to see Kaos again. The idea of being abducted before I could tell him that I didn't want to say goodbye made my pulse jackknife and my steps quicken. I didn't care if he didn't feel the same way or didn't know what he felt for me. I knew how I felt, and that was enough. If only I could make it out to tell him.

"He's trying to stop them from the cockpit," Erin said as she led us back the way we'd come. "Which means we need to haul ass before we get caught in whatever net of booby traps he's setting."

"That sounds like Daik," Val laughed softly.

We ran down one passageway and then another with Erin in the lead and Val wedged between us. When we turned again, Erin sucked in a breath and stopped short. Val and I both ran into her and then stumbled back, a few of the scientist's papers fluttering to the floor.

My heart seized when I saw the pair of Hettites at the end of the hall. They were wide enough so each one should take up the narrow corridor, but they were jammed in shoulder to shoulder. There was no getting around the corpulent aliens as cruel smiles split around their yellowed tusks. The thought of them taking me again made the blood in my veins turn to ice.

I took a step back, pulling Val with me as she grabbed wildly for her papers. Then a guttural growl from behind made me turn.

"Ducking hell," Val gasped.

An enormous, bear-like creature towered over us, his shaggy head brushing the high ceiling. When I noticed the pink tinging the tips of its fur, I released a breath. I spun around and pulled Val and Erin down as the transformed Tyrria leapt over us and tore into the screaming Hettites.

When the two aliens were a limp, bloody mass on the floor, Tyrria morphed back into her regular form and turned to us. Thundering footsteps were loudly closing in on our position, no doubt running toward the shrieks of their crew mates.

"Run!" Tyrria yelled as the ship shuddered again.

We ran, even as the sounds of chasing Hettites grew louder, drowning out the unmistakable sound of another ship locking onto us.

CHAPTER THIRTY-NINE

Kaos

I jiggled my leg as the Vandar ship locked onto the Xulonian ship containing the females, and I tossed my blade from hand to hand as I waited for the hatch to open. Skard, Naz, and Carly stood alongside me, and each looked as on edge as I felt. Behind us were Vandar raiders with their battle axes drawn, as eager to exact vengeance on the slavers who had worked in tandem with the Xulonians as we were. Tails swished rapidly in anticipation.

Dark thoughts zipped through my brain—Kensie dead on the floor with a blaster wound scorching her chest, Kensie being dragged away from me with a weapon held to her temple, or even worse, Kensie already gone from the vessel.

I tried to hold the vision of the woman with curly, brown hair in my mind, telling myself over and over that she would be unharmed. I would be on time to save her.

I'd cursed myself the entire journey to intercept the ship and the Hettite ship attached to it. How had we let this happen? How had I allowed Kensie to be in danger again? I was angry that I'd been so focused on the battle that I'd ignored the obvious danger to her and all the females, but I was more furious at myself for the way I'd left things.

If something happened to Kensie after I'd curtly bid her goodbye... The memory clenched my gut like an iron fist. Why had I been so quick to let her go when I knew it was the last thing I wanted? Just because I thought she didn't want to travel with me to my own time?

A deadly purr shook my chest. I hadn't even asked her to come or told her that I wanted her to be with me, no matter where I was in time or space. Instead, I'd held onto the old betrayal that I'd nursed for so long it was like a silky poison on my tongue. But Kensie hadn't betrayed me, and she hadn't deserved my cold dismissal, and now she might never know.

I swallowed down a knot of regret that burned my throat like acid. I refused to accept that I wouldn't find her. "Our story was written in the stars," I said under my breath. "It does not end today."

The steel hatch swung open. I rushed forward, the drum-beat of my heart keeping pace with the thundering footsteps around me. We'd locked on to the opposite side of the ship from where the slaver ship had attached itself, but it was only moments until we came onto a group of thick-necked Hettites. I remembered them from the arena, and my lip curled at the sight of their tusks and the rolls of skin hanging from them.

With a roar, I attacked and drove my blade into the nearest enemy before he could raise his blaster to fire. Around me, blaster fire erupted, and blood splattered the gray walls. Kalesh Naz leapt through the air and pounced on a Hettite, plunging a blade into the back of his neck and then landing in a crouch as the alien hit the floor in a lifeless heap. He raced off, and I followed him as Skard and Carly continued to slay the alien invaders.

I ran in tandem with my kalesh. It felt good to be back by his side, even if we were both racing to find our mates. As soon as the word entered my mind, I knew it was true. Kensie was meant to be my mate, just as Tyrria was intended for Naz. Kensie might not know it yet, but she was my one true mate, and it was my duty to prove it to her.

A piercing, female scream cut through the air and chilled my blood. Naz glanced at me, his jaw tense, and we powered forward with even more determination.

Rounding the corner, we stumbled over a pile of bodies. For a moment, my stomach lurched, but then I realized they were Hettite corpses. I lifted my gaze, and my breath caught in my chest.

At the other end of the corridor, Kensie was slumped against the wall beside Tyrria. Blood was smeared on the pale-gray floor around them, but it was impossible to know who it belonged to. Both females were sitting up, their arms wrapped around each other and their eyes open.

Naz let out a strangled cry and rushed to them. I watched as my kalesh reached Tyrria and knelt beside her, whispering to her as he brushed her pink hair from her eyes.

For me, time froze, and my body stopped moving. My legs became like lead, and it was impossible to take a breath. Every fear I'd ever had of losing love again slammed into me like an iron hammer. I'd opened my heart to Kensie and envisioned a life with her, but now that was being snatched from me again.

Time slowed as I fought against the choking terror of losing the one taste of happiness I'd had since I'd left Taor. I didn't know if I'd survive another heartbreak or if my soul would simply shatter. Kensie was meant to be mine for life, and I was already hers. I knew that now. I forced myself to take a breath and confront my fear. Fate would not be so cruel to snatch love from me a second time.

All this happened in the heartbeat before Kensie looked up at me, and her gaze locked on mine. When she smiled, the last dark dredges of fear drained from me, and I snapped from my arrested state. I returned her smile and watched her face transform with joy, but before I could draw another breath or run to her, pain exploded across my chest.

Naz whirled from where he knelt on the floor beside his mate, his face twisted in shock as a Hettite staggered into view and fired his blaster again. This time, the enemy warrior's aim went high, and Naz lunged at him with his blade. My kalesh plunged it into the broad belly of the creature, who gurgled dark blood from his mouth before dropping to the floor like a stone. Then Naz turned to me.

I clutched my chest as the pain made my legs wobble, the realization that I'd been hit spreading like the burning sensation in my body. Naz caught me before I collapsed, but even though he was holding me, it wasn't his face I saw before everything went black. It was Kensie's, as she stared at me from across the corridor. And it was filled with agony.

CHAPTER FORTY

Kensie

My skin was like ice as I watched Kaos grasp his chest and gasp. He'd been perfectly fine moments earlier, but then the blaster fire had emerged from seemingly nowhere and exploded across his shoulder. Despite my shock and horror, I couldn't scream as the burly Hettite fighter lumbered into the doorway firing wildly. All sound was snatched from me as I watched Kaos go rigid and lock eyes with me.

His expression was pained, but I knew it was more than physical pain that was consuming him as he stared at me. I'd seen that look before on Mick's face. It was regret and sorrow. He knew he was leaving me, just like Mick had, and, once again, I wouldn't have a say in it.

The Taori kalesh stabbed the Hettite so quickly I barely saw the flash of the blade. Then he was lunging for Kaos and catching him before he fell to the floor.

Still, I couldn't move or speak as Kaos' sad gaze held mine before his eyes rolled back into his head and he went limp.

"Is he—?" Tyrria asked, her voice cracking as she practically crawled to where Naz cradled his first officer's body on the cold, steel floor.

A wave of nausea swept over me at the thought of losing someone else I loved. Had I really cared so much about leaving my own time that I would have given up the chance to finally have what I'd lost? Had I actually let fear convince me that hiding my heart would keep me from getting hurt again? I almost laughed at how absurd that now seemed. I could as soon have stopped myself from loving Kaos as I could have stopped him from rushing headlong into battle to save me.

Then my chest hitched. I loved him.

As terrifying as that was, there was no denying it and no more running from it. The idea of losing Kaos was scarier than the idea of risking my heart, and I cursed myself for only realizing that now that I might have lost him. Tears burned my eyelids and burned my vision as I held my breath.

"He is not dead." Naz pressed a finger to Kaos' neck and then lowered him to the floor.

A strangled sob escaped from my lips as I made my way over to him, my hands slipping on the blood coating the floor. "He's not?"

Naz ran his fingertips over his first officer's scorched chest, the skin between the dark ink flushed red. "His heartbeat is strong, and the hit was not direct."

I placed my own hands over his firm chest muscle, smearing blood on his hot skin but being reassured when I felt the steady thumping of his heart. Then I bowed my head over my hands and let the tears flow. My shoulders shook as I let go of all the pain of losing Mick and all the struggle to keep myself from ever experiencing that again. I sobbed as the thick walls that had kept me from allowing myself to feel anything finally crumbled to rubble, and I embraced the pain as I knelt over Kaos.

"You are getting me wet."

Kaos' soft burr of a voice made me open my eyes and lift my head. His eyes were only slits as he stirred, but his cheeks were dotted with my tears.

"You're alive," I managed to rasp.

"And wet."

My sobs turned into laughter, as I swiped my tears from his face. "I thought I'd lost you."

He opened his eyes fully, the iridescent blue shining brightly. "I thought you did not choose me. You wished to remain in this time without me."

My heart fluttered, the familiar fear of rejection and loss resurfacing, but I pushed past it. "You didn't ask me to come with you."

His heart stuttered beneath my hands. "And I am not asking you now."

My head swam, and my throat tightened. What had he just said? "You aren't?"

He gave a small shake of his head as he pushed himself onto his elbows. "I am telling you. You are coming with me."

I opened and closed my mouth without speaking.

"We aren't meant to be apart, Kensie." His voice was husky as he lifted a hand to cup my face. "True mates never are."

I swayed and let my face rest in his palm, relief making me dizzy. "True mates. I like the sound of that."

Kaos' gaze narrowed then raked from my face down my body. "You are not well."

I shook my head as he sat up fully and ran his hands over

me, pausing at the sticky side of my shirt. "I'm fine now that you're here, and we're going to be together."

Kaos lifted my shirt and sucked in an agonized breath. "You are wounded."

I glanced down at the gash oozing blood from my side. I'd been so busy worrying about Kaos that I hadn't even noticed the throbbing pain in my side until that moment.

"I tried to fight them off as a Drendalen scorpion, but they got off a shot before I reached them," Tyrria said, smothering a sob with her hands.

I looked at Tyrria and noticed a bruise blooming on her cheek, a gash, and a scorch mark on her arm. She hadn't emerged from the fight unscathed, but her gaze was riveted to the blood pooling around me.

A Vandar raider raced in and skidded to a stop. "We've eliminated the last of the Hettites." He took in the sight of us on the floor, and he jerked his head back. "Bring the female to our healer if you want her to live."

Kaos seemed to be strengthened by the sight of my injury. He lifted me and stood in a single motion and then hurried behind the Vandar as I wrapped my arms around his neck, just as I'd done on the alien moon. And just as on the alien moon, I sensed I was safe with him.

"You're carrying me again," I murmured.

"I will always carry you, mate," Kaos said as we left the sound of Tyrria's sobs behind us.

I met his gaze. "Always is a long time."

"It will not be long enough with you. My soul has always been yours, and it will remain yours until it crosses into the shadowland."

I let out a content sigh. That was what I had always wanted. *He* was what I'd always wanted but had never allowed myself to hope for. I allowed myself a smile as I faded away.

CHAPTER FORTY-ONE

Kensie

I rolled over and burrowed my face into a warm chest. My fingers splayed across firm muscle as a deep sound buzzed my fingertips. I opened my eyes and tipped my head back to see Kaos peering down at me.

My heart pitter-pattered at the sight of him. I was still adjusting to the reality of being with the Taori and officially being his mate. Even though he'd told me his feelings when I'd been drifting out of consciousness after the Hettite attack, I'd made him tell me again once I was fully awake. I'd loved hearing it both times, even though the huge, gorgeous, devoted alien seemed too good to be true. I sometimes felt like pinching myself, but Kaos was real, and he was mine. Just like I was all his.

"Did I wake you?" His velvety whisper feathered across the top of my hair.

I laughed and drummed my fingers on the darkly inked skin of his collarbone. "You were growling."

He looked abashed but then his own lips quirked into a smile. "You insist on sleeping naked."

As if this was all the excuse he needed, which, maybe it was.

"After being in the Vandar sick bay for way too long, I want to be able to sleep completely relaxed."

Kaos propped himself up on one elbow, his expression becoming stern. "You were not in the med bay for too long. It was necessary for your injury to heal."

I instinctively touched a hand to the thin scar on one side of my torso. Aside from leaking plenty of blood, my gash hadn't damaged any internal organs. I was certain I could have left the strict Vandar healer's care earlier, but Kaos insisted I be fully recovered.

"What about your injury?"

He shrugged. "I told you. I am Taori. I have suffered much worse."

"Show off," I muttered, even though I'd seen for myself how quickly he'd recovered from being shot by a blaster and had to believe that his claims about Taori strength weren't all bravado.

"There was no place for you to go even if your injury hadn't needed tending," Kaos continued. "The Xulonian ship needed to be repaired after the Hettite attack and refitted for our journey through time."

I scanned our new quarters, which were noticeably larger than the original compact rooms. The Taori first officer and I now shared a large bed along with a round dining table for two and a pair of chairs. There was even an alcove in the far wall, with a fake fire crackling away. Apparently, this was a suggestion from Raas Ronnan, and was implemented in all the new couples' quarters. It still wasn't as sumptuous as the arena complex, but I'd take it any day.

"I have to admit that I'm impressed by how quickly you got the old enemy ship converted into your new sky ship."

Kaos grunted. "It isn't a Taori ship, but all the Xulonian technology we're taking back with us makes up for the fact that it was designed by them."

"When Val stopped by to visit me on the Vandar ship, she said that she was able to use the Xulonian tech to figure out how to create the artificial temporal wormhole."

The Taori nodded. "They had the ability to move through space, which is how there was a wormhole opening so close to their planet. It was a remnant of one of their past experiments. They were so xenophobic they never wanted to use the knowledge."

"Their fear is our gain." I hesitated before asking my next question. "What's left of them, anyway?"

Kaos ran a hand through his black hair, his fingers bumping his horns. "Most of their population survived but they have none of the technology that once powered their cruel moons. All their manufacturing ability was destroyed, their flight capability was obliterated, and the collective that controlled the planet was eliminated."

I gulped. "Do you think they'll survive?"

"They were told why their planet was punished, so maybe they will be able to reflect on the price of their cruelty and abuse of others. If not, there are enough of our remaining allies to ensure the Xulonians do not rise again and repeat their actions."

"Val said that her fellow researchers were found on the Hettite slaving ship, along with another imperial security officer."

"They were being saved to be released onto the moons."

Kaos's face twisted in an expression of disgust. "Now they will stay here and join the others in ensuring something like this never happens again."

"I'm guessing Erin and her resistance pilot boyfriend are leading the group?"

"She and Ty have already left to tell the Novaya resistance that they are alive, and about what happened here."

I felt a pang of sadness. Erin had come by the med bay to tell me goodbye, but it was sad to think that I'd never see the woman again—or taste her impressive cooking. Even so, I knew she was eager to get back to her undercover work with her hot Neebix boyfriend.

I swallowed the lump in my throat. "And the Vandar?"

"Raas Ronnan and his horde continue their journey to find the other Vandar." He sighed. "We owe them a debt we can never repay."

"Especially since we won't be in their time." I patted his chest. "I wouldn't worry about it. I get the feeling they're the kind of alien warriors who love a good fight." I scrunched my mouth to one side. "Who else do I know like that? Hmm..."

Kaos gave me a crooked smile. "Maybe you are right about that. It was an honorable battle."

"And now we get to leave the Xulonians behind forever."

The Taori made a gruff sound in his throat. "Except for their ship."

I shrugged. "It's totally revamped. It barely looks like it used to. I heard that Lia even did a Filipino cleansing ritual to get rid of the Xulonians' bad energy."

Kaos wrinkled his nose. "The corridors still smell like the herbs she burned."

I shook my head with a laugh. "Better than the smell of sweaty warriors."

Kaos cocked a dark brow. "You do not like the way I smell?"

I grinned, moving my hands down his body to the top of the dark skull emblazoned on his chest and stomach. "Actually, you smell good enough to eat." To prove my point, I leaned forward and dragged the flat of my tongue across his skin.

He groaned. "Kensie."

"What?" I used my most innocent voice. "You know I'm fully healed."

Since my injury, Kaos had been treating me like I was made of glass. Although I loved the way he pampered me and insisted on taking care of me, I wanted more.

"But, your wound..."

"Is completely fine," I argued. "You have worse scars than this. I've felt them under your tattoos."

I traced the curve of his inked skull with the tip of my tongue, provoking another tortured moan. I pulled back and gave him a wicked smile. "I want you inside me. I *need* you."

His jaw was clenched, as if he was trying to restrain himself.

I twitched one shoulder as I moved down his body, wrapping my fingers around his cock, which was thick and rigid. Kaos' eyes popped wide as I fisted the base of his cock and its broadest crown, although my fingers didn't come close to touching. Winking at him, I brought the top of his cock to my lips.

Kaos raked both hands through his hair, this time clutching his own horns and lifting his eyes to the ceiling. It was fine with me if he wanted to fight it. I didn't mind a good fight.

With a moan of my own, I spread my lips around his crown and took him into my mouth, savoring the incredible feel of his skin and the warm, musky taste of his skin. I swirled my tongue around him and hummed as he thickened even more under my touch.

"Goddess of the moon," he gasped through gritted teeth.

I felt a thrill as I worked my mouth up and down his substantial shaft, taking as much of his length as I could. He might be the huge, alien warrior, but I was the one making him powerless now.

With a growl, Kaos pulled me up, flipped me onto my back, and crushed his mouth to mine. My protests were swallowed by his claiming kiss, his tongue moving against mine with a drugging rhythm. Then he was pinning my hands over my head and parting my legs with his knee.

Before I could catch my breath, he thrust inside me, filling me completely with a single, hard stroke. His mouth swallowed my scream, which almost instantly morphed into groans of pleasure as he started to move inside me.

This was different from when we were in the storage room and sweat was rolling off him as his fever ravaged him. This wasn't as fast and frantic, although there wasn't a moment of doubt that he was fully claiming me.

Kaos tore his mouth from mine and locked his gaze on me, our eyes so close I could almost feel the brush of his eyelashes against mine. The brilliant blue of his eyes had been devoured by the black of his pupils, which flared as if lit from within by a molten fire.

"So perfect for me," he murmured. "As if you were made for my cock."

Each of his hard thrusts took my breath away and made me unable to speak. Kaos rolled us both over again so that I was on top of him, straddling his hips with his cock still buried inside me. He gripped both hands on my hips and lifted me up, his gaze going to where our bodies met. As he drove me down on his cock, his pupils darkened. "You take me so well."

I arched my back, thrusting my bare breasts into the air as

he worked me up and down his length. Heat suffused my body and blood roared in my ears.

Then he was parting me and circling his finger around my clit. No, not his finger. I dropped my head so I could see the dark tip of his tail moving between my legs as he drove me down on his cock again and again.

My eyes rolled back in my head at the overpowering sensations, as my body began to quiver. I put my hand over the furry tip of his tail, guiding it between my legs and pressing it down until my body jerked wildly, clenching around Kaos as I threw my head back and scraped my hands down his chest. I screamed his name as my pussy spasmed, barely aware of his own guttural sounds as he drove himself deeper into me.

I fell forward onto his sweaty chest as he gave one final hard stroke and pulsed hot inside me with a roar. I waited for his cock to swell and hold me to him, but then remembered that his fever was broken.

"No clench," I managed to say between stolen breaths.

His own breath was ragged, and his chest rose and fell, lifting me up and down like a cresting wave. "No clench." He wrapped his arms around me, spinning me under him again. His eyes flashed and he licked his lower lip. "Which means I don't have to stop."

I blinked at him in surprise, startled that he was still hard inside me. "You don't need a break?"

He tilted his head at me. "Why would I need a break?"

Oh, boy. I released a breathy sigh. "You Taori really *are* immortal."

CHAPTER FORTY-TWO

Kensie

"I think we should all raise a glass to Val!" Tyrria said, as she retrieved a bottle of alien wine from the cooler in the galley kitchen.

To celebrate making it through the artificially-created temporal wormhole and landing in the correct time—give or take a few astro-months—the females on board were having an impromptu gathering. Carly, Val, Tyrria, and I stood around the counter as Lia searched for glasses.

"I never had any doubt you'd do it," Lia said, clapping as she found a collection of mismatched glasses in a cabinet.

Val smiled and tried to wave off the compliment. "I had a lot of motivation. I didn't want to end up blown up or flattened like a pancake."

Carly's eyes widened. "Was that a possibility?"

Lia laughed as Tyrria popped the cork off the bottle and

poured it into five glasses. "It doesn't matter, because Val did it. We're back in the original Taori time and reunited with the rest of their sky ships. And we only had to use the anti-Quaibyn serum on one of the guys. I'd call that a massive success."

"The other Taori were shocked when they saw us." I shook my head as I recalled us being introduced as the mates from the future and the stunned looks on the other Taori warriors.

"Not that they'd say a thing against your guy." Carly nudged Tyrria.

The half-Kayling half-Lycithian gave a smug smile as she lifted her glass. "It pays to be banging the kalesh."

We all burst into laughter, and I put an arm around Tyrria's shoulders. She'd come a long way from the day she'd arrived in the battle arena complex scared and unsure.

Lia held her glass high. "To Val, for getting us here in one piece."

We all clinked glasses and drank.

Carly gasped after chugging her glass. "What the hell was that?"

I couldn't disagree with her. The wine had a kick like a donkey without a hint of sweetness. I made a face and put my own partially full glass down on the counter.

Tyrria pulled the bottle closer and eyed it. "I guess it's Xulonian wine?"

We all made faces.

"First order of business is going to be tossing out anything Xulonian," Val said. "I, for one, don't want a reminder of those guys."

Carly leaned her elbows on the counter. "Do you think they're already assholes?"

"What?" Lia asked.

"It's five hundred years before we encountered them. I

wonder if they're already on a path to being the horrible aliens they end up being."

Val held up her hands. "If we start messing with the future—"

"Too late," Tyrria said. "Us being here has already changed the timeline."

Val frowned, which meant she knew Tyrria was right. "That still doesn't mean I want to track down the aliens who hunted me."

Carly put a hand to her stomach. "That booze did not sit well with me. Do we have anything to munch on so I can get rid of the taste of fermented dog hair?"

Lia giggled. "I wouldn't mind some bread. I've had a dodgy stomach all morning."

"Same," I said. "It's probably from our trip through the wormhole. Didn't you say it could have some effects on us?"

Val nodded. "Nausea isn't an unusual side effect."

Tyrria opened the lower cabinets searching for food then she opened the cooler again, handing out containers with unknown contents.

I peered at a cylinder filled with a ruddy brown substance. "I wish Erin had labeled her creations. I have no idea what any of this is."

Carly expression contorted in a brief pang of regret. "I'm going to miss that girl—and her cooking."

Lia squinted at a square container with suspicion. "We definitely should have thought through having someone come back with us who could cook."

I opened the cylinder I was holding and took a tentative whiff. My stomach roiled in response, and I dropped it on the counter. "Ugh. It's some kind of fish."

"I love fish," Val said, retrieving the container I'd dropped, and then turning green and pushing it away. "Never mind. Not that fish."

Tyrria slapped a hand over her nose. "How does that smell so bad? It can't be old. I watched Erin make it just before she left and we jumped back in time."

"Maybe the wormhole altered the food?" Carly suggested as she held her nose with one hand and tried to get the lid back on the container with the other.

"Maybe we're the ones who're altered."

We all turned to Val, whose eyes were wide.

My pulse fluttered. "What do you mean? I thought the trip would be harmless. Are you saying that it changed our sense of smell? Is it permanent?"

Val put a hand on her stomach. "I don't think it altered our sense of smell. I think we were changed before we went through the temporal wormhole." A nervous giggle escaped her lips. "And, yeah, I think it's permanent. At least the results are."

Carly glanced at the rest of us. "Does anyone know what she's talking about?"

We all shook our heads except for Lia who sucked in a sharp breath. "It can't be."

"What?" Carly practically yelled.

"Val thinks we might be pregnant," Lia said in a hushed voice. "Right?"

We all stared at Val and then at the offending fish, as if it was the reason we all had a heightened sense of smell and nausea.

Carly shook her head. "No fucking way."

I instinctively pressed a hand to my own belly. "I didn't think you could get morning sickness so quickly."

Val shrugged. "We don't know anything about Taori pregnancy. Maybe carrying a Taori fetus gives us super-sensitive smell early."

"That would explain why I can smell Torst before he enters a room," Lia muttered. "Not that it's a bad thing. I like the way he smells, but lately, I could track him by the scent of his skin."

"All of us?" Carly looked around at our group.

I cleared my throat as my face warmed. "That mating clench had to have some purpose, right?"

Tyrria held up her palms. "There must be another explanation. When Kaylings get pregnant, they get a line of pink dots along their hairline. I might only be half, but I'm sure I would show signs."

Val peered at her. "I hate to be the one to tell you, but—"

"You've got pink dots!" Carly shrieked.

"What's going on in here?" Kalesh Naz's voice made us all jump and turn to the door where all our Taori mates stood.

"We could hear you down the corridor," Daiken said, stepping inside and curling an arm around Val.

She gave him a shy smile. "We just realized something."

"We're pregnant," Carly blurted out.

Skard's jaw dropped. Torst locked eyes with Lia. Kaos didn't move.

"All of you?" Kalesh Naz asked, his voice almost a whisper.

I nodded, and all the other females joined me.

Before I could speak, Kaos had swept me into his arms and buried his head in my neck. Around me, there were laughs and excited murmurs.

"I didn't think I could be happier than I was," Kaos whispered into my hair, "but I am."

I released a sigh of relief. "You're not freaked out?"

He pulled back. "My true love is having my baby. What could make me happier?"

"I suggest we find a planet that hires out nannies," Carly said. "This ship is about to get very loud."

"But first, we get rid of that fish." Lia pointed to the container.

"Does this time have Alluvian cream ices?" Tyrria rubbed her stomach.

The Taori exchanged confused glances.

I laughed and patted Kaos' chest. "I take it that Taori females don't have food cravings when they're expecting?"

He shook his head. "I've never heard of any."

Carly laughed at Skard's shocked expression. "Strap in, boys. It's going to be a wild ride."

THANK YOU FOR READING STORM! If you loved the Taori (and were intrigued by the Vandar), be sure to read more of Raas Ronnan in PRODIGAL!

> "Prodigal was impossible to put down and I absolutely loved every page of it!"-Amazon Reviewer

One-click PRODIGAL>

This book has been edited and proofed, but typos are like little gremlins that like to sneak in when we're not looking. If you spot a typo, please report it to: tana@tanastone.com
Thank you!!

Also by Tana Stone

Warriors of the Drexian Academy:

LEGACY

LOYALTY

THE SKY CLAN OF THE TAORI:

SUBMIT (also available in AUDIO)

STALK (also available on AUDIO)

SEDUCE (also available on AUDIO)

SUBDUE

STORM

Inferno Force of the Drexian Warriors:

IGNITE (also available on AUDIO)

SCORCH (also available on AUDIO)

BURN (also available on AUDIO)

BLAZE (also available on AUDIO)

FLAME (also available on AUDIO)

COMBUST

The Tribute Brides of the Drexian Warriors Series:

TAMED (also available in AUDIO)

SEIZED (also available in AUDIO)

EXPOSED (also available in AUDIO)

RANSOMED (also available in AUDIO)

FORBIDDEN (also available in AUDIO)

BOUND (also available in AUDIO)

JINGLED (A Holiday Novella) (also in AUDIO)

CRAVED (also available in AUDIO)

STOLEN (also available in AUDIO)

SCARRED (also available in AUDIO)

ALIEN & MONSTER ONE-SHOTS:

ROGUE (also available in AUDIO)

VIXIN: STRANDED WITH AN ALIEN

SLIPPERY WHEN YETI

CHRISTMAS WITH AN ALIEN

YOOL

Raider Warlords of the Vandar Series:

POSSESSED (also available in AUDIO)

PLUNDERED (also available in AUDIO)

PILLAGED (also available in AUDIO)

PURSUED (also available in AUDIO)

PUNISHED (also available on AUDIO)

PROVOKED (also available in AUDIO)

PRODIGAL (also available in AUDIO)

PRISONER

PROTECTOR

PRINCE

The Barbarians of the Sand Planet Series:

BOUNTY (also available in AUDIO)

CAPTIVE (also available in AUDIO)

TORMENT (also available on AUDIO)

TRIBUTE (also available as AUDIO)

SAVAGE (also available in AUDIO)

CLAIM (also available on AUDIO)

CHERISH: A Holiday Baby Short (also available on AUDIO)

PRIZE (also available on AUDIO)

SECRET

RESCUE (appearing first in PETS IN SPACE #8)

All the TANA STONE books available as audiobooks!

INFERNO FORCE OF THE DREXIAN WARRIORS:

IGNITE on AUDIBLE

SCORCH on AUDIBLE

BURN on AUDIBLE

BLAZE on AUDIBLE

FLAME on AUDIBLE

RAIDER WARLORDS OF THE VANDAR:

POSSESSED on AUDIBLE

PLUNDERED on AUDIBLE

PILLAGED on AUDIBLE

PURSUED on AUDIBLE

PUNISHED on AUDIBLE

PROVOKED on AUDIBLE

BARBARIANS OF THE SAND PLANET

BOUNTY on AUDIBLE

CAPTIVE on AUDIBLE

TORMENT on AUDIBLE

TRIBUTE on AUDIBLE

SAVAGE on AUDIBLE

CLAIM on AUDIBLE

CHERISH on AUDIBLE

TRIBUTE BRIDES OF THE DREXIAN WARRIORS

TAMED on AUDIBLE

SEIZED on AUDIBLE

EXPOSED on AUDIBLE

RANSOMED on AUDIBLE

FORBIDDEN on AUDIBLE

BOUND on AUDIBLE

JINGLED on AUDIBLE

CRAVED on AUDIBLE

STOLEN on AUDIBLE

SCARRED on AUDIBLE

SKY CLAN OF THE TAORI

SUBMIT on AUDIBLE

STALK on AUDIBLE

SEDUCE on AUDIBLE

ABOUT THE AUTHOR

Tana Stone is a USA Today bestselling sci-fi romance author who loves sexy aliens and independent heroines. Her favorite superhero is Thor (with Aquaman a close second because, well, Jason Momoa), her favorite dessert is key lime pie (okay, fine, *all* pie), and she loves Star Wars and Star Trek equally. She still laments the loss of *Firefly*.

She has one husband, two teenagers, and two neurotic cats. She sometimes wishes she could teleport to a holographic space station like the one in her tribute brides series (or maybe vacation at the oasis with the sand planet barbarians). :-)

She loves hearing from readers! Email her any questions or comments at tana@tanastone.com.

Want to hang out with Tana in her private Facebook group? Join on all the fun at: https://www.facebook.com/groups/tanastonestributes/

Cover Design by Croco Designs

Editing by Tanya Saari

Printed in Dunstable, United Kingdom

66110489R00133